Black Tie Affair

Blackstone, Volume 4

Rachel E Rice

Published by Millennium Books, 2024.

Black Tie Affair
By Rachel E. Rice
Copyright 2015 by Rachel E. Rice
Re-edited in 2023

Table of Contents

Alex

"Yes, he is the most indecent, delicious, handsome, arrogant man; his blue eyes circled with dark lashes, and when he stares at me, a hot wave of desire surrounds me, covering me, taking me away into his arms, where I forget I'm married to Maximillian Blackstone, the love of my life."

Blog: www.rachel-e-rice.com[1]

<u>Newsletter</u>[2]

Prologue

When I first met Maximillian Blackstone, I thought it was the day I took an offer for employment at his hotel in Montana, when ours eyes and then our bodies merged. He sauntered into the Millennium Lodge with his entourage, dressed in a tailored black suit, and black shirt with the collar opened displaying his taut chest. His stride slow and deliberate, taking in everyone around him with a hint of a smile, a handsome man if ever I saw one. His serious gaze with dark hooded eyes under those long full eyelashes concealing his exceptional green eyes, then connected with mine.

However, I discovered it was earlier that I first crossed his path. I entered his orbit on the morning of my interview as he exited his Manhattan building. The impressive structure displayed large gold-plated letters with Millennium written over the portico. When he strolled through the chrome glass door to his black limo our eyes connected for a moment as quick as a flash of lightning on a spring day. No warning. Just that fast, and then he disappeared into the limo and behind the black windows.

Passing him as I entered the building, in those seconds, I felt a pull weighing me down. It was a strange feeling, where I had to shake my head, then turning catching sight of his back entering his car. His short dark curly hair revealed a fresh haircut. His shoulders wide, with that

---

1. http://www.rachel-e-rice.com

2. http://eepurl.com/4uh-b

black suit fitting impeccably close on his body. The suit not wearing him, but he, wearing the suit as if part of his skin. His long legs and expressive manicured hands stood out when he turned with his eyes acknowledging me, and those gold cufflinks catching the sun bouncing off and holding my eyes as he passed in those seconds.

I entered the glass doors, hoping for a position at one of Blackstone's companies. At the time I needed a job and I would accept anything they offered. I took the thirty-third floor to Max's office building waiting for an interview, unaware my life would change. When I passed him and he glanced at me it was because he recognized his selection.

It was all coming back to me. The folder held by the woman from HR with the black business suit, not so sensible shoes, and the blonde hair, dropped important information about me on her desk, which was the key to my past and the key to my future.

A past of adoption, a past of homelessness, and fear. Fear of graduating from college and not having a job and a place to stay, and mounting school debt, which had sustained me through college because by now my sponsor had cut off my funds. When I accepted employment in Montana at Max's swanky ski lodge, I had never been to that state, and never been on skis. I was anxious to get out of Brooklyn for a short time, so I accepted the position because of the outrageous money offered for a few months' work.

But if they were giving it away, I said, "What the hell, I'll take it." I could learn to ski and pay some bills.

Off I flew, and that was the day my life changed. I married Maximillian Blackstone after loads of drama, with the kind of drama and kinky stuff only found in movies. A marriage proposal from my birth mother's husband, then the pregnancy, and finally a marriage proposal from Max, which I eagerly accepted because I loved him, and I was tired of fighting him for custody of our son.

Unpredictable and exciting was just one reason I said, '*I do take this man...*' I had never seen a man as handsome as my Max. I could see him now with his expensive Italian bespoke black suits and white shirts and ties. His shoes made just for his feet. Dark curly hair and those green eyes. Just thinking about him could bring me to a state of unequal sexual pleasure.

I didn't really know this man then and what he was capable of doing, and I still didn't, and he didn't know me. *Does anyone really know anyone or what they are capable of?*

All I desired at the time was to be in his arms and to have him make love to me in whatever manner suited him.

Chapter 1
Alex

Out of sheer boredom and curiosity, I reached for one of the local New York papers and read the headlines aloud while sipping a cup of coffee. "Socialite found bound, gagged, nude, and dead wearing handcuffs. She was discovered by her husband with her arms trussed over her head and fastened to a white velvet headboard in her Park Avenue apartment. Nude and dead," I repeated.

Sounds like the first time I met Max when he deserted me and didn't call. I felt dead when I thought I would never feel him inside of me ever again.

"A five-hundred-dollar light pink printed silk chiffon scarf tied neatly around her neck." *It escapes me why a reporter would put the price and description of the scarf. Am I missing something here?*

Raising my head, looking around, shaking my head, and taking another sip of coffee, I continued reading.

"Her lover explained, 'it was all a game,' when the police questioned him. 'Ask the husband, he knows, he was watching,' quoted the lover. 'His voice dry and matter of fact as if he was inconvenienced by my questioning,' Detective Munro said during a press conference."

"How is this news?" I threw the paper across the room. "Is that all they can write about? What's news about a woman finding pleasure in having a lover and her husband watching them in bed?" I murmured to myself. *What's the world coming to?*

Maybe it's the dead part that people find distasteful and newsworthy.

Then a thought crossed my mind, *This woman could be me in a few more years if I don't do something besides wake up in the morning, get dressed, and wait for Max to summon me.* Maybe he'd come tonight, maybe tomorrow. *Who knows?* I was a perfect candidate for the front page:

Wife of billionaire Maximillian Blackstone arrested for flogging her naked lover and holding him as a sex slave: *"I haven't had sex with my husband in months and my nerves were on edge. The sexiest man alive has traded me in for an even younger woman. I'm barely twenty-four, and because of lack of serious sex, and boredom, I found a lover I could handcuff to my bed and flog him senseless if he didn't perform,"* Mrs. Blackstone confessed to the detective. News at eleven.

That would make for great headlines if I had nothing to live for, but I did.

It was raining in New York and I was looking down on Central Park. *What am I doing here anyway?* It was my stupid idea to move to New York. I must be crazy. I convinced Max that I would be happier in a city. I would see him during dinner when the children were awake, sometimes. After that, your guess would as good as mine when the next time he'd show his face. And a gorgeous face at that. It had been two days since he came home and called. I knew he had an apartment a block away that he used for sleep. I promised him I wouldn't cling. He had been under pressure with Charles making bids on his properties, and he was not wanting to sell.

After Max broke up my wedding to Charles, Charles hadn't forgiven me or him.

I leaned forward, looking out with my legs extended on the chaise lounge, trying to count all the people walking. The fog was rising, obscuring my view. They were little dots like ants.

I was happy when Max asked to marry me. I married him because I loved him, and he understood my rebellious nature. I was beginning to think that the only reason he married me was because of the children, and he couldn't accept losing me to Charles, or wanted anyone to have me.

He could be like that with people and things he desired—like his properties and me. I guessed he considered me his property. Me, the children, and the dog. He was like a child with toys. He didn't want anyone to play with his toys, even though he would not play with them. He hid his favorite toy in the closet, and maybe pulled it out when he tired of it, or stumbled on it by mistake.

That was who I was in this marriage. Max's favorite toy he hid and buried for later.

That reminded me, we were running out of toys and lubricant, not for the children, but for us.

That was me—Alexander Bishop Blackstone, his Domme for the day, wife for a lifetime, and who the hell knew what the next minute. All I knew was he hadn't been in me for a week. This coming from a man who liked to possess my mouth every day, initiate a light spanking, and give me hard penetration at least every other day, but now it had been months since we had old-fashioned vanilla sex. And it'd been a month since he'd even mentioned the bondage thing, where he was naked wearing a blindfold. Or was it me wearing a blindfold? I forgot, it had been that long.

I *feel like a caged bird. I want to fly*. I turned and looked and in scurried my little dog, and he jumped on my lap. He'd bought us a miniature dog, a Havanese, because he knew we would be left alone. It was Max's way of giving us something to do to keep me and the children occupied. The poor little thing thought I was his mother. He had serious separation issues. I told Max that it was too soon to take it from his mother.

Max had said, 'Disappointments and pain was in everyone's future.' Just because he and Jonas lost their parents early was no reason to deny the puppy his experience with his mother. Max just looked at me with his dark brooding hooded eyes, and said, 'It is what it is. It's done.' What he meant by that was left to interpretation. I'd say he was back to his old controlling indifferent behavior.

The little puppy would probably have issues, like I had issues, and like Max and Jonas had issues. That reminded me I needed to make an appointment to see a therapist. It was my idea to consult a sex therapist this time for me and Max. Our relationship was suffering because I had children. Max had this problem before. Something about seeing me as a mother instead of his sex partner.

The little dog was nuzzling up to me and sucking my finger. He thought it was his mother's tit. I'd better feed him. The children would be getting up soon.

THE RAIN STOPPED AND the nanny took Maxim and our baby, Jack, short for Jackson, out to the park to play with the other rich overprotected children. I was surprised that Max even allowed it. He finally gave in when I explained to him that they would be misfits if they didn't have time to play with other children their own ages.

He suggested that we go back to his ranch in Montana where they could have horses and dogs. 'Children learn a lot from animals,' he had said. I wouldn't hear of the idea, and he brought in a lovely honey brown and white miniature puppy. I didn't want the quiet of Montana because I felt that Max wanted to isolate me. We always had divergent opinions. He wanted a rural life, I wanted urban, and now never the twain should meet.

Our personalities always clashed. I thought now we were only staying together because of the children. I hoped not.

It was time for Havas to go out. We both needed fresh air. I grabbed a blue jean jacket and tossed it over my shoulders to complement my worn jeans and white tee shirt. I clutched the leash in my hands and tugged on it as the dog trailed behind, and when we were out the door, he scampered in front of me, heading for the elevator. It took time for the elevator to get to our floor because the penthouse was twenty-five floors up.

Max said that I should take our private elevator, but I squashed that idea. It was enough to have to isolate myself in this gigantic apartment building, but not seeing the few tenants that came through here, now that would be pure hell. So, I opted for the elevator where I could at least meet someone. It had been months and still I got on the common elevator alone.

Finally the elevator stopped. I was full of anticipation. The door opened and all I saw was this gorgeous undeniably handsome man standing in front of me. He had on a pair of faded jeans and a white shirt and soft-brown-leather jacket. He was all of six two, with a wicked gaze and the bluest eyes. It was like looking into an endless ocean. His hair ruffled as if he'd passed his fingers through, or some woman had raked her hands through it when they were in bed, and he'd never bothered to comb it. He strutted to the side to make room for me. I smiled inwardly, knowing what I could do to him.

I would handcuff him to his bed, sit on his face and take a handful of that beautiful shiny black hair, and yank all that long dark curly hair as he gave me an orgasm. Then I would have turned around and faced that hard dick, because by now it must be hard, and put my full mouth over his penis and sucked the come from his gorgeous body. I would leave him weak where he couldn't move. Then we... I caught myself dreaming about that handsome man. Max was driving me crazy with his sexual neglect.

Max started me on this road to mind-blowing sex and now that's all I can think about.

Since I'd been with Max, I found myself daydreaming about men. I gave a small smile and he shot me a nod, with a mischievous curl of his lip raising on the right of his face.

His smile lit up my body and made me feel alive. "Beautiful dog," he said to me. I stepped into the elevator locked on his eyes, and was caught by surprise by his strong soft and easy voice. It had a melody to it as if he could talk you to sleep. A bedroom voice.

"Yes, it's a beautiful dog." I was caught by surprise when I heard a woman's voice. I looked to the side and near him with his wide chest and taut body hiding her, a woman about twenty stood punching the button incessantly to get the elevator to close.

"Something is wrong with this elevator. It always takes us to the top floor," she said. He gave her a passive glance, her eyes lowered. "When are you going to get me a dog? I want one just like that," she purred at him. And she stepped to the right side of the handsome man and grabbed his hand. I stood in front of them, and I could feel his eyes trailing down my back, causing chills to explode over me. I wanted to run, but there was no place to go. Sweat accumulated under my arms, and warmth pooled between my legs.

I thought I was only attracted to Max, but this man registered off the scale. "Do you live here?" he asked, his voice deep and sensual.

The pretty model who was about six feet looked him in the eyes and then her glance turned to me with contempt, and she said, "Can't you see she's an employee. You are embarrassing her."

I went along with the folly and the blonde with the expensive clothes and Chanel purse. "I work for the Blackstone's. I'm their sometime nanny and dog walker," I said with a smirk. The model with the highly developed cheek bones, long legs, and skinny frame, said, "See, I told you." And she felt very satisfied with herself.

When the door opened, I stepped out. I could feel those steel-blue eyes ravishing me, I lowered my head, and his girlfriend trailed behind me. The doorman wasn't sitting at his desk. He took his break early, but the cameras were filming. I was glad he wasn't sitting there, because I didn't want him to blow my cover by calling me Mrs. Blackstone.

I felt satisfied in my deception.

Opening the glass door, I gave a sigh of relief after I got clear of that hot body. I put the dog down and the little dog stopped at a garbage basket to sniff it. That gave me the opportunity to turn my gaze to my left just slightly, catching sight of his confident alluring stride, his black limo parked at the curb, and the driver standing near the open door. The model slid in and he looked my way and our eyes connected. I lowered my head, trying not to be too obvious, but I felt it and I know he did too. He smiled entering the limo, but that smile was for me, not the model.

I knew that look too well.

I couldn't function for thinking about him. I took the dog to the park and watched his aimless pursuit of squirrels. Heading back home, down Park Avenue, I stopped off at the deli to buy Max a tin of caviar. He liked having a snack before dinner and wine. He needed his gold or crystal spoon to eat it along with roasted potatoes. I never could get use to those fish eggs.

"A five-ounce tin of your finest Ostrea caviar," I said to Ralph.

"Sure thing. It just so happens we have it today, grade one golden," he smiled, pointing to the five-hundred-dollar tin of Russian caviar.

"Your employer makes you pick up his snack food?" I stiffened. I recognized the voice. It belonged to that impossibly handsome man with the expensive jeans, expensive jacket, expensive white shirt, expensive shoes, expensive face, and expensive smile. I didn't know why he made me nervous, but he did. Could it be because I was afraid that I could fall for him? The answer was a straight-out *yes*. I could fall naked all over him, and especially on that handsome face.

"I volunteered," I said turning around, meeting his sexy gaze with a raised eyebrow, and I turned back to Ralph who stood waiting patiently behind the counter, and said, "Put it on the bill."

"Sure thing," Ralph said to me.

I spun around with a stern face looking him in his impossibly blue eyes, and said, "What are you doing, following me?" He didn't answer for a moment. He looked at me from my feet on up, and said, "I would follow you to the ends of the earth and then back again." That did it. This was getting too strange.

"I don't think we have any more to say to each other." He just stared at me with a secretive smile, which made him the second-hottest man alive. After getting my package, I rushed out and he headed behind me.

He stood in front of me, "You know we recognize our own." *What did he mean by that?* I asked myself. What did he recognize about me that I didn't already know? That I was over-sexed and didn't know it until I met Max? That I was desperate for that feeling again and that I wasn't getting any lately?

"I don't know what you mean, and you are wrong on all fronts if you think I know what you're talking about," I said to him, and hurried along with my dog in one hand and my package in the other. He had me so nervous that I rushed to my apartment, nodded at the doorman who made his appearance, and now was sitting behind his desk smiling at me.

"Hello, Mrs. Blackstone. Nice weather we're having." Clearly he hadn't seen the downpour, and the gray skies that were signaling that summer was over. I looked around and there was no sign of my stalker. I rushed into the penthouse elevator at the far end of the lobby and hurriedly put my key and code in, and slipped into the safety of my home.

Chapter 2

"Ms. Blackstone, the children ate and took their nap. They're tired from all that running up and down in the park," Lapita said, heading in the direction of the kitchen, then turning and stopping. "Oh, Mr. Blackstone called." My heart skipped. *Why does it do that when I hear his name?* "I told him you left your cell phone here, that's why he couldn't get in touch with you. He said that he'll call you later, or text you if he can't get home tonight."

Handing Lapita the dog, I hurried to take a shower and change out of my clothes. The weather was cooling, but my temperature was rising, and I had sweat dripping from my hair to my lower body. I dropped my clothes, stepped over them and headed for the shower. I needed a shower for more than one reason. I felt sexually frustrated. Max hadn't made love to me and performed his incredible oral sex lately. My sexual cycle had been messed up.

I was used to a routine with Max. First the oral sex, then the vanilla, then the anal and a little kink with the anal beads. Our sexual lives had been full, but a lot was lacking now since we had been in New York and had a new baby.

Now I wanted what he had initially introduced me to. I begged him to tie me up and pleasure me. I wanted to feel him in my mouth, in my opening, inside of me filling me. I wanted his body close to me all over me, skin to skin. It was Max who turned me into a raven sexual lunatic, and now he was missing in action.

Reaching and turning on the hot water, my body came alive. I placed two fingers on my folds to simulate the feeling I received from Max. After a few minutes, I gave up on the self-stimulation. This didn't make sense. I was too young to even consider this. I hated him and I loved him at the same time. "You are the one who has made my life a living hell," I accused Max. Yet I didn't mean it. I wanted him and I needed him.

Max had explicitly stated in our marriage contract that I should never masturbate without him.

Turning facing the shower door, I saw a shadow standing in my bathroom. The figure strutted in the direction of the shower. "Max. Where have you been? I thought you weren't coming tonight. I thought you were out of town." Turning off the shower, I opened the door and rushed into his arms, drenched in water, dripping on his expensive black suit. He grabbed me pulling me to him and holding me in his arms. All the sexual tension melted away leaving clay to be molded by him into whatever he desired that moment.

He grabbed a handful of my wet hair and turned my face up to him. He kissed me with all the promise of what I'd missed. His tongue fought for control of my mouth and it won. I surrendered and let it take over.

He stood back, his eyes poring over me and down to the hair on my mound. "You make me so hard when you don't shave. You know I can't stay away from you for long." He took off his tie, threw it on the floor and unbuttoned his shirt. Then he strode to me and went to his knees. He lifted his head back and pulled my body to his face. I felt his finger enter me. I felt his tongue swirl around my clit, and I heard his moan.

His moans laced with pleasure, deepening my arousal. He kept his finger inside me, and slowly inched it in and out. "Alex, what am I to do with you?" he said, raising his face looking at me, before resuming his claim of my body. "I feel so complete. I want you day and night."

"I love you too, Max. I can't get enough of you," I said breathlessly as he worked his magic on my clit, but as I was saying this, the face of the second-most-handsome man in the world flashed through my mind. *What the fuck!* I thought. *Why am I thinking of him? I'd better get to the therapist and soon.*

"Max, I didn't want to come so soon," I said breathing hard, my mouth wide. "I'm coming and I can't help myself." I slid my hands through his hair and fisted it, pulling it with every release of juice from my body on to his heavenly tongue and lips.

"Turn around," Max commanded, "...and face the wall." I wanted him so badly that I obeyed his command. He took a latex out of a drawer near the sink, then opening the wrapper, he placed it near me. Max unzipped his pants as his eyes glared into the mirror, his eyes greedily roaming my body, settling on my mound. He stepped out of his shoes, his pants, his underwear, and he threw his socks across the room. He walked close behind me, I could feel his hardness, his fullness, and the heat. "I want all of you tonight," he said to me.

I knew what he meant when he said those words. "That's all we have been doing lately," I said, counting the colors in the wallpaper, waiting for that jolt from his hard penis to invade my body, sending me into an erotic frenzy of pleasure and a quick orgasm once more.

"I don't want you to get pregnant again. Our baby is barely a year," he said, pulling in and out of my butt cheeks. He was right. Two children and I never thought I would have one. Let alone two. Then he took a step back and lightly spanked my butt. Then a hard whack. The sudden surprise caused me to tighten up and then he slammed into me.

It hurt at first even with the lubricant, but once it was in it felt glorious. I met his thundering motion, leaning my butt into him as he gripped my hips with his hands. He pulled out as if teasing me, and made a circular motion on my butt before plunging further, until he hit a wall and couldn't go any further.

"I need this and more," he said, breathing loud into my neck, and with each warm breath, every inch of my skin exploded and opened.

"Quiet, we can't, we have the boys and servants, remember. You must be satisfied with this in the bathroom," I said in a whisper.

"I can't wait, and I don't like when you tell me no," he said with a firm abrasive voice.

"I'm not telling you no, Max, I'm saying wait until we are in the apartment. Then we can do whatever we need to do." His breathing was hard, his manhood stiff. He rocked on me until he reached his orgasm. I felt him fill my cavity.

That was his first. When he was in a sexual frenzy and passion brought on by stress, he could have as many as four or five before he went limp, and I'd never seen him limp. I learned why he needed the Bondage and S&M, because regular vanilla sex couldn't satisfy his insatiable sexual desires. I really didn't think one woman could satisfy him. Yet he made himself content with what we were doing, but I didn't know how long he could last with just me, and that scared me to death, making me feel insecure.

What troubled me more was my attraction to that handsome stranger who was now interfering with my marriage and sexual life with Max, or was it me?

I had developed an out-of-control sexual appetite, and that scared the hell out of me as well. Maybe I was laying the blame everywhere but where it belonged.

He walked away and dropped the used latex in a basket and entered the shower. After his shower, he stood staring at me lying waiting for him. He lay on the floor, and I crawled over him as he spread his legs. "I need you to tie this around your eyes," he said, handing me a silk black ribbon. His hands slid through it making a snapping sound. I didn't ask him why he walked around with it, because I was so happy to have him home, and inside of me. That was my ribbon he took from me a year ago. But wait. He was doing everything to me except making love to me.

Looking up at him and not saying a word, I tied the black ribbon over my eyes, and he said, "I need your mouth. The way I taught you." I couldn't see him, but I knew he was looking at me. I held his penis tight in my hands. Then my mouth made a circle around it slowly. I licked it carefully at first, and then he put his large hands to my face, and said, "I command you to suck me the way I know you can." What was I doing? I didn't feel the arousal the way I had before.

Could it be because of that man? The one that made me quake when he was around, and he was always around in my mind neutralizing Max's control over me.

I tried again blocking him out, and soon I was in the rhythm, but I was unhappy with Max. I wasn't his sub or Domme, *I'm his wife dammit*. But what could I say, it was all part of the strange love life of the Blackstones.

I didn't blame him, but myself. I wanted him so badly that I agreed to marry him and partake in his games. We were not like a regular family. He owned homes all around the world, and two penthouse apartments, and an office building in New York. In our secluded apartment on the nightstand, there wasn't a clock to remind us to wake and go to our perspective jobs, but a clock that timed our erotic interludes.

Seven o'clock, tying me to a bed and spanking me, then fucking me. Eight o'clock, reach for the lubricant and insert it in my cavity to make his anal penetration pleasurable to both. Nine o'clock, tie him to the bed, or handcuff him and whip him until he came. Ten o'clock, he experimented with anal beads and various toys on me, which caused him to come over and over.

That was my life, and somewhere I lost myself. But did I want to find me again, was the question?

As usual he would drop wherever he was, take a nap, and start again. I placed a blanket over his beautiful naked body and closed the door. At least he was home. Some women had men that drank and they ended up on the floor and covers got thrown for a different reason. *At least he is with me now*, I thought. *What happens if I can't keep up? Will he discard me and the boys for someone who will?* Although I was now married and had rights, I was still insecure.

Insecure because I had two sons for a controlling sexual billionaire, who would never let me go unless he didn't want me anymore.

How did you get a grip on a man who was like a mountain with no edges to hold on to?

He was still a beautiful handsome man in his thirties, and I was still that twenty-something who was a runaway, homeless, and feeling like a child to a mother I never knew, who was dead and had given me away, and a stepfather who wanted to marry me because I looked like my mother. I guess I was as fucked up like Charles St. John, my stepfather, who was out to ruin Max because Max took me from him.

I reached for a silk robe, placing my arms in and then tying the belt around my waist. We had been having sex for three hours. Now it was time for dinner, and Max wouldn't miss another dinner with the children. The large glass and chrome table was set as Max had directed every day, the chef had prepared a meal of roast duck with orange sauce, and Max had his caviar and wine, and soft music to calm the savage beast inside him.

Walking out of the room heading for the dining area, I spotted a basket of long-stem red roses. I looked to the maid, "Did Mr. Blackstone bring these?"

"No, Miss." I bent down to pick up the card. There was nothing on the envelope, so I took the card out, it read:

To The Most Beautiful Woman,

I'm sure I will see you again. I will make it my life's work to find out your name. Until we meet again, which I hope will be soon.

Your Devoted Servant,

Robert

Your devoted servant? Was he making fun of me? Did he think I worked for Max? I knew I didn't get out much and maybe I should. I didn't want anyone to think that I was just Max's maid. He had a beautiful woman with him. Why would he want me? Did I look that vulnerable? I should get rid of him. *But do I want to?* I questioned. I liked the attention.

Chapter 3

Panic settled in. My eyes blinked over and over from the tension or coffee. My mouth twitched. I was nervous. What had I done to be nervous? Nothing. I just fanaticized about that incredible handsome man who seemed to think we had something in common, which we didn't. I was married to the most desirable man in the world, and this man, Robert, was an irritating handsome sexy cock hound. There was no way I was going to screw my life up engaging in an affair with him.

OMG why was I entertaining the idea of an affair? I grabbed the basket of long-stem red roses and rushed down the hall. I hid the basket in one of our guest bedrooms and then on my return trip, I bumped into Max.

"You're all dressed. Where are you going?"

He had a strange look on his face. One I had seen before when he didn't want to tell me his secrets.

"I'm flying out of town. I'll be back tomorrow. If I'm not back, then it will be next week."

"Oh, for Christ sake, Max," I said, turning away from him. He eased behind me and put his hands around my waist with his nose to my neck, his mouth warm and tempting.

"I explained to you, Alex, that it will take a lot of time from the family to sell all my properties. Then I will be home with you and the boys whenever you need me."

"Can't you call Jonas and let him help you."

"Not this time," he said. He released me from the warmth of his body and I felt alone once more. "I have to say goodbye to the boys." He kissed me on the head and walked to the children's rooms.

I turned, getting a glimpse of this beautiful man as he strode up to the second floor to peek at his boys, dressed in a black suit, with a white shirt, and dark silk tie. I smiled a reminiscent smile, recalling the first time I fell in love with him.

Making up my mind wasn't easy. I couldn't go on with this endless waiting and worrying, hoping Max would come home just so I would get a few hours of his time. I was determined to find something with which to occupy my time. I would either get a job or enroll in college. *That's it. I'll enroll in college and get my law degree.*

Max kissed me, and although he gave me several orgasms so I wouldn't miss him, I still felt empty and misdirected.

I had more than most women my age. I didn't need anything anymore. I had children, food, shelter, an education, servants, and the most beautiful handsome and desirable man on the planet, and still I was lonely and unfulfilled. I reached for the phone, called the therapist, and made an appointment for Wednesday at four.

————— ◉ —————

I DRESSED CASUALLY in black, but not too elegant. It bothered me to wear very expensive clothes. I found a pair of wool, cotton, and silk blend black slacks and a white shirt with cuffed sleeves, black shoes, and an expensive Louis Vuitton purse. The kind that you couldn't recognize as being one of those. I just felt that I had to splurge on something. Jonas had done well in his business ventures and Max no longer had to wire him money, so with the extra money he put in my account, I bought clothes, and things I didn't need or want.

I needed my husband's attention and I wanted him home with me at night. I began to question, *what kind of fucked up life have I accepted?*

The sex therapist serviced both of us. That was a strange choice of a word—serviced. It wasn't like we were getting a tune-up or maybe we were. We went separately and then we decided to go once a month as a couple. It had been working out fine until Max started missing his session and our session together when the discussion of our sex lives became the subject.

Max didn't have sex without anal sex, and I was beginning to crave it as well. I didn't know whether that was bringing us together or ripping us apart.

I began to question whether he was bisexual.

Dr. Wolff's office was very discreet. It was located in a building in Manhattan where doctors in different fields cared for wealthy clients. When you entered the building you couldn't figure out who was going to a gynecologist, oncologist, psychologist, or psychiatrist. His office was situated next to the oncologist.

I preferred people thought I had cancer than mental health issues. I felt there was less stigma in having cancer than sexual problems.

Entering the office of Dr. Wolff, the secretary greeted me with her usual professional closed-mouth smile. She was about fifty, dressed immaculate in a designer suit that may have been left over from the sixties. She appeared to be a pleasant sort and no doubt discreet. She was very proficient and wouldn't let a patient go over a minute without sending out a bill for an extra hour. Somehow you felt that you had to be there on time, otherwise someone would be sitting in your chair.

His secretary smiled and opened the door to his office. I entered the room and sat in the yellow leather chair. Like clockwork Dr. Wolff sat quietly waiting. He had a look of a listener, always shaking his head in agreement, but never saying a word until you had poured your soul out to him.

I placed my purse next to me on a table. He hadn't nodded at me yet to indicate that I should begin. I felt comfortable because Dr. Wolff was in his sixties, and he wasn't at all the type to play games, and he didn't make me feel like a child because I was in my twenties. I had tried out a few therapists before, and they were more interested in getting a boner listening to what I had been through with Max. So, I made an appointment with Max's therapist.

"We may begin, Mrs. Blackstone."

I sat nervously picking at a cuticle on my index finger, gazing at him, and trying to decide whether my secret was safe. Then I thought, *What the hell. If I can't tell him and trust him with my deepest secrets then who can I trust?*

"Dr. Wolff, I have a problem."

"Yes, Alex, I know. That's why you're here," he said, staring at me over his half-moon glasses.

"I met someone in my apartment elevator and I found myself attracted to that person. I have seen many men, and the only man I have ever felt that way about is my husband, Max. I am left wondering whether something is happening to our marriage. Maybe he's finding another woman attractive as well?"

"Does this new gentleman, he is a man, I assume?" After raising my eyebrow and staring at him, I shook my head yes. "Does he view you in the same light? What I mean is, is he attracted to you?"

"He sent me flowers. I led him to believe that I was an employee of Max and not his wife."

"Did you do that because you wanted him to think you weren't married?"

"I don't think so, but maybe," I said hunching my shoulders, wondering about my intentions, and reaching for the truth, which existed somewhere in my subconscious. If I lied, then these sessions would be a waste of time.

I stayed the full hour with questions about Max's sexuality and my love life. Mostly me complaining that Max and I weren't having vaginal intercourse. In the middle of revealing all the anal stuff, his secretary knocked and walked in, and said it was time for his next client, and he would be there soon. I stood, retrieved my purse, smiled, and exited through another door.

I knew he wouldn't forget where we left off, and he would have answers for me next time.

Dr. Wolff's clients came in one door and left out of another door so they wouldn't meet. I left the office feeling relieved and smiling. Reaching for the button, the elevator door opened. I stepped back to allow people to exit, but to my surprise, the man I feared stood before me. My mouth parted, there stood that smiling gorgeous seductive man who was not my husband, but someone I would consider sleeping with in a minute, if I wasn't married to the sexiest man alive.

He stood with his hand on the elevator door, preventing it from moving. "After you, beautiful woman of my dreams." I looked up at him stunned and speechless. I slid under his arm and smelled his sexy just-bathed scent. It had been weeks since I'd smelled a man like him. It had been weeks since I'd smelled Max's body after a shower.

"Damn, you smell good," he said to me with words I wanted to say to him. "That perfume is two hundred a bottle. You're no dog walker, Mrs. Blackstone."

"How did you know?" I asked, my eyes narrowing and my lips in a hard line, angry that he had found me out and called me on it.

"I didn't, but when I see someone that makes me feel the way you make me feel, then I have to take notice and I find out everything there is to know about them."

"Now that you know who I am, and that I'm married, I hope we can just be friends."

"There is no way we can just be friends. You see, we are alike in so many ways," he said, smiling and showing all his white predator's teeth. When he made that remark my eyes narrowed out of curiosity, waiting for him to say more, then I spotted a security guard hurrying in our direction.

"Oh it's you, Mr. Montgomery. I thought the elevator had gotten stuck again."

"I'm getting on the elevator," I said looking at the guard, and throwing a glance in Robert's direction. "That's his name. Robert Montgomery," I murmured. The card on the flowers he sent said

Robert. Now I had one piece of the puzzle. My hands trembled as I rode the elevator down to the main floor. I never experienced such nervous and crazy unexplained feelings before, except when I first met Max. I was relieved when the elevator door closed. I could still see his dark-blue eyes following me, as if he and I shared a dirty little secret.

And we probably did. Thank goodness we couldn't read minds. But I could read his face and he was dangerous. Not in the sense of bodily harm, but dangerous to my marriage.

——●——

I MADE IT HOME IN TIME to be disappointed once more. A text message came in from Max: ***Can't get home today. Had to fly to Hong Kong.***

Love U.

Another night alone. There were only so many books and romantic novels I could read before I began to feel as if the characters were having more fun than me. I tossed my latest romantic novel on the floor. *I must get out of here,* I thought. I hated to go anywhere alone, but tonight I would risk it. There was a bistro at the corner of Park Avenue just down the street from the Penthouse.

Maybe I should interview my driver there. Max said I could have my own driver. I rushed to the bedroom and located the number. I sent him a text and told him to meet me at 560 Park Avenue at nine o'clock. He responded—Okay.

I ate dinner with the children, put them to bed and showered and dressed in a little black dress with a black leather jacket. I wore my black and white Jimmy Choo's with the ankle straps. I hurried to the bistro I had passed once on a shopping spree. The waiter saw me standing nervously waiting and sat me at a small table for two.

It was a small upscale stylish quaint restaurant with French themes. Candles lit on the tables covered with what appeared to be handmade tablecloths. Colorful copies and posters of Toulouse Lautrec pictures hung on the wall, a picture of the Moulin Rouge and an assortment of nudes. The French singer Edith Piaf's singing *La Vie En Rose* drifted seamlessly in the background giving a mood of times gone by.

I ordered a cognac. That was Max's drink of choice. I tried getting into his world with the caviar and the wine and now cognac. I discovered that I could sip it without drinking much, but my tolerance for liquor was low.

The smell alone could render me drunk, but it gave an air of sophistication to sip and swirl the brandy snifter. I looked around taking in the quant bar, with its old-fashioned style and European charm. My eyes wandered, then settled on the back of a man sitting, waiting with a drink in his hand. His hair showing an expensive cut, his shoulders wide, his legs long, and I recognized him. Was he following me? Apparently not, because in a few minutes of my gawking at him, in walked a sultry blonde with legs that never stopped. She was taller than he by maybe an inch. Six feet three would not be a stretch to say the least.

I watched as she gave him a kiss on the lips. The kiss lasted a few seconds, then he stood and wrapped his long arms around her waist. He waved to the waiter and the waiter showed them to a table across from mine. I tried to slide down low in my seat, but to no avail. There he was facing me when he pulled out her seat, and the model-slash-hot-chick had her back to me when his deep blue eyes locked on me like a programmed armed missile.

What is going on? I questioned fate or nature. I couldn't seem to step out of my door without running into that exquisite man. When his eyes caught sight of me staring at him, I saw his hands tremble. I knew I had that effect on my Max, but never had I experienced that with a stranger.

He nodded his head, and Edith Piaf's rendition of *Autumn Leaves* set the stage for what happened next. Before he sat, he smiled lightly and winked at me. The young woman thought she had garnered that sexy smile with those incredible white teeth, but it was me he saved that suggestive smile for, I knew it and I would never forget it.

But I needed to forget him.

When he sat down he ordered for both. It was not the same woman I saw in the elevator in my building. Clearly he controlled the situation. Clearly he had no trouble in the romance department. Why was he after me? His eyes would wander to me to the point that the young woman turned to see what had caught his attention. She met my gaze. I gave her a quick smile, lowering my eyes, and hunching my shoulders from embarrassment. I heard her say he was rude for not paying more attention to her.

He never reacted or changed his devouring gaze focused on my mouth.

Chapter 4

When I took my second sip of brandy, in walked a man in a dark-blue suit and white shirt casually opened, young and good looking, eyes clear blue. I informed a woman at the employment agency to send me someone with stamina because he would be on call twenty-four hours, but I never imagined she would send a hunk of this magnitude. He stopped and asked the waiter something. The waiter pointed and he headed in my direction.

I saw a tinge of jealousy wash across Robert's face. I noticed because of his new haircut that the tip of his ears flushed red when the guy stood in front of my table.

I gestured for him to sit, and he smoothly pulled the chair out and sat down. His long legs extended to the side.

"My name is Brandon Dewild, my agency said that you will need a driver on call twenty-four seven." I held out my hand and he shook it. His handshake not too strong and not too firm, and yet it had a sense of authority with it.

"My husband suggested that I hire a driver, but I only need one part time."

"I was expecting at least eight hours of employment, Mrs. Blackstone."

"Oh, I will pay you for the full eight hours, but you will only work a few hours a day and maybe weekends. If I can make some kind of arrangement with you for your services when I need you, I would appreciate that."

Robert stopped his conversation with the model and leaned in to hear what I was saying to Brandon. Why was he listening to my conversation instead of paying attention to that beautiful girl? "Would you like a drink?" I asked Brandon.

"Oh no, Mrs. Blackstone." He shook his head. "I never drink when I'm with a client."

That appeared to go over nicely. Because he was a handsome man, with a full head of dark-blond hair, I found myself smiling more than usual. He was certainly a charmer. I asked him unnecessary frivolous questions. I asked him if he had a family, a wife and child, to which he reported that he did not, but he did have one interfering sister. I knew how old he was because I had his folder setting in front of me.

"Where do you live?"

"I live in midtown," he continued talking, providing information that he thought I wouldn't ask because I wanted to be polite, or because I was new at this. "I have an apartment with my sister who just came up from Nebraska to go to school. She wants to be a clothing designer one day."

We had a round of small talk, and then I said, "Are there any questions you would like to ask me?"

He looked at me, and said, "Will your husband have a problem with me as your driver?"

"No. He's the one that insisted on me hiring one."

"I know, but you and I are about the same age. I'm twenty-four and..."

"How did you know?" I asked Brandon.

"I Googled you," Brandon said to me.

"Then you know as much about me as I know about you."

"I'm afraid so. When someone is as rich as Mr. Blackstone, their lives are an open book."

"I hope I can trust you to be discreet."

"If you hire me that is usually in the contract. In any case it will not be a problem," he said with a shy wavering smile.

I looked up and Robert was standing and leading his blonde model out the door. He turned before letting the girl walk through the door and winked at me, or it appeared to be a wink. Maybe in the dim-lit bar I saw something that didn't exist. It was that way when a shadow cast a light across an object. That was why you could never believe anything you saw. Except my eyes didn't deceive me, Robert was as handsome and stunning as Max, and he made me feel something deep down inside that was now absent in my relationship with Max.

I concluded the interview, shook Brandon's hand a second time, and said, "Report for work tomorrow at noon." I had plans to do a little shopping and I shouldn't forget to call my good friend, Joshua. It'd been too long since we'd talked. I hadn't seen him since Crystal dumped him for Max's twin, Jonas.

Crystal left off with Jonas, and the last time I heard, they were getting married. But knowing Jonas, it would be a cold day in hell before he did. He was too flighty and he had serious mental issues. Nevertheless, he had been stable with Crystal. She must have been good for him and kept him out of trouble.

My thoughts were interrupted by the soft voice of Brandon. "Mrs. Blackstone, would you like me to walk you to your apartment? Or I can call you a cab." I turned in my seat facing him, looking up into his big sincere trusting eyes.

"I like to walk. And I would appreciate the company." I paid the tab and Brandon stood and took my hand and I stood. We walked along Park Avenue with its expensive properties and shops. Max owned two of the buildings, and as we looked up the insignia of **Millennium** could be seen for miles. His offices were at 504 Park Avenue, not far from our apartments. What was I thinking to marry a man like him? Too much money and not enough time.

Here I was taking a leisurely walk with my driver and not my husband. Everything was wrong with that picture.

"We're here, Brandon." The doorman opened the door when he saw us. I smiled at the doorman as we walked in.

"Thanks, Brandon, I'll see you tomorrow around 10 a.m. You can pick up the car then. I'll show you around our garage. I don't like limos. The Bentley will do nicely for me."

He had a smile on his face. I guessed he didn't like limos either.

"I'll give you an allowance for you to buy some new suits and whatever you need. Don't forget at 10 a.m."

"How could I forget? This is the beginning of the best job I've ever had," Brandon said with a wide smile, making my day, and I was sure his. Finally, someone my own age to talk to.

I stood watching his nervous reaction to me, as he placed his hands in his pocket, straightened his collar, and quietly waited for me to speak. He made me feel young again because we were the same age, and it was good talking to people my age. *I need to get back to college. I* thought. *I need to socialize, maybe go to a bar, and get drunk.*

I shook his hand and he turned, heading outside and leaving me standing in the lobby. He waved when he walked out into the crisp cool evening air. Brandon looked back and I waved and through the open door trotted that impossibly eye-catching man. I turned quickly and scooted to my elevator, trying to avoid him. I stood at the door in the corner and fumbled in my purse for the elevator key.

When I finally found it, I stuck it in the lock, but a hand covered mine. The intense feeling of his touch shot in between my thighs making them quiver with need. "So, we meet again," he said with a hoarse sexy voice and a broad grin.

I turned gazing into his big blue eyes. "I have to go," I said breathing hard and fast.

"I just want to say that I saw you watching me." I turned to face him, furious.

"I wasn't watching you," I said. "You were facing me, I couldn't help seeing you. You should have given your date your full attention. Instead your eyes were on me," I said, livid because he was so observant, or I was so obvious. "I think you were following me," I said, lacing my voice with icy contempt.

"Does Mr. Blackstone know that you're hot for me?"

My mouth opened and I stood in shock. "Are you out of your mind?"

"Yes. Over you," he said in an erotic whisper. I was speechless. The door opened, but he had positioned his body in front of me and blocked the entrance. "When are you going to give me a chance to get to know you?"

"I'm married..." I said, my body unsteady. His eyes locked on mine and he could feel his effect on me.

"You know if I kissed you and made love to you, you would leave Blackstone tomorrow."

"Why not today," I said to him. He leaned in to kiss me and I leaned back with eyes blazing. "Why you presumptuous ass. You're pretty sure of yourself." I bit my lip and murmured, "Cocky bastard."

"Yes, that I am," he said. "I know you, and I know your husband. Remember when I said that we know our kind. You are frustrated. Blackstone is neglectful. You have always been true to him, and he doesn't realize what he has. If you were mine, I would keep you satisfied every minute and never let you out of my sight."

"That's your problem. No woman wants a man to shadow them day and night."

"But they want a man to satisfy their sexual desires, and I know that Blackstone has introduced you to a certain way of life, and he's neglecting you."

"How do you know that? Wait, don't answer that. It's enough. I don't care to continue this conversation with you." I realized that I had given him too much information by just talking to him. I should have avoided him at all costs, but I didn't. I questioned my motives. Why didn't I stop this?

"It's your choice, beautiful lady." He moved out of my way before cocking his head to the side and shooting me a grin with a little taste of laughter, which showed the predator that he was. And my body, boiling, burning, red-hot, scorching, and not even Max could put out the fire that was smoldering white hot within me, and soon could ignite and burn down the Blackstone Empire.

Chapter 5

I rushed into the elevator out of breath. He was the most obscene man I had come across since I met Max. I had to find out who he was, because I was at a disadvantage not knowing anything about him, but clearly he knew me and Max. I tried Googling him and nothing came up. Maybe I hadn't gone back far enough. Wait, he's about Max's age—thirty something. Let's see. It struck me, I whispered, "Let me Google tenants in our building on Park Avenue." And there it was, his picture and what a picture.

Clearly he was a ladies' man. Every page filled with him and a different women. His name, Robert Montgomery, and he was a lawyer, and businessman like Max. *How curious!* As I scrolled through trying to glean some idea of what kind of man would stalk a married woman, the doorbell rang. I shut down my laptop, planning on returning later. "What now? Didn't Lapita hear the door?"

I walked quickly to answer the door. The doorman was taking his usual breaks and didn't call up to notify me of a visitor. I opened the door, and the doorman stood with a basket of yellow roses with a judgmental expression. An eyebrow raised. "Who are they from?"

"Mrs. Blackstone, I just make the delivery." He handed me the beautiful basket overflowing with an assortment of long-stemmed roses, placed it on the floor at the entrance to my foyer, and he stepped outside and went about his way.

"What now?" I exhaled and opened the card. Another present of roses. I bent to smell them, and there was a key hidden inside the envelope. My breathing deepened.

I read it: ***When you want someone to satisfy you and there is no one, I can give you what you need.***

Holy shit. How does he know what I need? Am I that transparent?

"Oh fuck me," I murmured. This was getting out of hand. Should I tell Max? "No!" I shouted into the empty room. I had answered my own question. *He's so jealous. Who knows what he could do. At least I still have my freedom. I can go where I want.*

I focused on the note. What did he mean? He couldn't know anything about Max's needs for BDSM. Or could he? Only I was sure of this, but then I couldn't be sure of anything anymore. I reached for the phone and called Crystal. I needed to talk to Jonas.

"Hello."

"Crystal. Is Jonas there?"

"Who is this?" Crystal said with a tense desperate voice.

"It's me, Crystal, Alex."

"Oh, Alex, I was thinking of calling you," she said with a whine. "I made a big mistake getting pregnant for Jonas. I thought Jonas had changed." Crystal went on and on about her problems with that twin brother of Max. Once Jonas took Crystal from my friend, he was satisfied. Then he began to neglect her to indulge in his demons. Sounded like someone else I knew.

After listening to her and agreeing with everything she said, I gave her a few sympathetic and encouraging words, "Jonas loves you. I will speak to him. Have him call me when he returns."

"Okay, Alex, but don't tell him I discussed our personal life with you." I hung up the phone and instead of throwing the key away which Robert deliberately sent me, I placed it in my jewelry box.

⬥

GETTING LITTLE SLEEP because I didn't have Max's warm body next to me, I woke early and dressed, had breakfast with my boys and Lapita, gathered them up with the little dog in tow and took them to their favorite place—the park for an hour. I expected Brandon at eleven.

I promised to show him the garage and let him take the Bentley out to get acquainted with it. After a shower from all that running around after the children, I dressed in tailored black pants and a white shirt. The doorman rang my bell and announced that my driver had arrived. I said to the doorman, "Have him wait for me in the lobby." Rushing out into the hall, searching through my bag, making sure I had my keys, I hit the wrong elevator button, and it opened immediately.

"Don't be afraid to get in here with me. I won't tie you up and take you in this elevator, although I'm tempted. I want your full cooperation, Mrs. Blackstone," Robert said, shooting me a sinister grin and a wink together with his expensive smile.

I felt warm sensations travel throughout my body. My legs grew weak.

I should never have gotten on that elevator, but I had to prove a point, and that was, I wasn't afraid of him. "Do you always talk to married women that way?" I stared him down. "Suppose I was to tell my husband, or better yet call the police and tell them that there is a sex fiend lurking in the elevators in my building."

"Do as you like. They won't believe you and they may take you to jail. The mayor and police commissioner are friends of mine."

"Why? Are you some important man who can't be touched?"

"I'm a man who knows secrets and keeps them," he said with a dark stare.

"My husband happens to be a very important and powerful man, and if..."

"But you won't," he said looking at me with those dark secretive blue eyes. He stood with his legs crossed and his arm leisurely propped against the wall of the elevator, calm, and at ease. Like nothing could touch him and he could do whatever came to his mind and no one could stop him.

"Don't you ever work?" I asked.

"Funny you mentioned work. I'm on vacation," he said with a smile that could lay waste and warm even the coldest of women.

"You must have enough money to go somewhere," I said.

"What are you trying to do? Are you asking for a ride on my yacht to my secluded island?"

"That will be the day."

He pretended he didn't hear me. His glance took me in from my head to my feet, settling noticeably on my lips. "Not today, I have a date," he said lightly. And he stood back with a cocky smile as the elevator opened. He nodded and waved his hand for me to exit. I glanced at him with a raised eyebrow and hurried off the elevator, and he strolled behind me. Feeling his eyes on me, I stopped and turned, and then I spotted Brandon standing with his arm propped on the security desk. I had never been so happy to see anyone.

Robert passed me turning around just long enough to show Brandon a bold disapproving glance, a raised eyebrow, and his lips tight.

Brandon ignored him. "Have you been waiting long," I asked Brandon.

"No, Mrs. Blackstone."

"Don't call me Mrs. Blackstone, call me Alex. You and I are the same age." We turned and headed for the elevator to the garage.

"Mrs. Blackstone, it looks better if I keep a distance between us. And if you don't mind, I think I'm going to like this job, and I want to keep it." The elevator stopped. "After you, Mrs. Blackstone."

We walked into the garage. The third floor contained all Max's cars. He had about ten, maybe more. There were three Bentleys, two dark blue ones, one convertible, one hard top four door, it was the one I wanted Brandon to drive me around Manhattan. I adored the dark blue Bentleys.

I was getting used to this life with all the toys. We passed his Porsches, one red and one gray four door that I hadn't seen. I remembered him telling me when I felt like going to the Hamptons we could ride in it for the weekend. So far we hadn't traveled anywhere, and I hadn't seen our home in the Hamptons.

After passing two Lamborghinis and two limos and one Aston Martin. "Finally," I said, "This is the one you will drive." Brandon's face lit up like a little boy with his first train set.

He opened the door and I hopped into the back. Brandon walked around to the driver's side whistling. I was happy someone enjoyed and got use out of the cars. The car wasn't outfitted to be driven by a chauffeur and I liked that. As Brandon drove out of the garage, waiting to cross at the light stood Robert and another one of his little friends. "Let him go, Brandon." Robert passed in front of the car with a different girl headed for his apartment. This one was a brunette, slightly smaller and slightly younger.

He stepped in front of the opened garage door, investigated the car and stared as if he could see me behind the tinted windows.

"A friend of yours, Mrs. Blackstone? I don't mean to be forward, but he looks like he admires you."

"Admiration is a wrong choice of words, Brandon. That's not admiration on his face."

"I was being respectful, Mrs. Blackstone. I know men very well. Please, be careful."

"I tell you what Brandon, I get nervous when you call me, Mrs. Blackstone. I could never get used to that greeting. When we are riding or when no one is around, please call me Alex."

"Okay... Alex."

"Good. Do you have a car?"

"No, Alex," Brandon said, as if practicing feeling comfortable calling my name. "I have a bike and motorcycle. It's too expensive in this city what with insurance and parking garage fees. It would cost more than my apartment."

"Which did you ride today?" I said making small talk, glancing at him in the mirror.

"I chained my bike outside the building."

"When you want to ride your motorcycle, just leave it in the parking garage. I'll text you the code."

"Thanks, that's generous of you, Mrs.... I mean, Alex."

"Stop in front of Bergdorf Goodman. I should be there for one hour. Just some light shopping." Brandon stepped from behind the wheel. I tried to act like I was comfortable having a chauffeur, but after being homeless since I was a teen, *Well, you can put a saddle on a mule and say it's a racehorse and it will still be a mule.* In other words, I wasn't comfortable in the role of a billionaire's wife either.

Just as I stated I was out in an hour. "You haven't eaten, Brandon, do you want to go to lunch?"

"Mrs. Blackstone I hate to turn you down, but I'm not your friend, I'm your employee. As I said, I like this job and I like you. We could both get in trouble if Mr. Blackstone sees that you are being familiar with the help."

"Brandon, you let me handle him."

"To make you feel better, I've eaten. I will eat after class."

"Do you go to college?"

"Yes. New York University. I'm a film student."

"Wow. That's great." We sat quietly listening to the radio, One Direction was playing, and then we reached the building on Park Avenue, my self-imposed prison, I felt sad and I felt anxious. Sad that I didn't have Max with me and anxious about Robert.

I waited in the car as Brandon stepped out and opened the door. I was doing this as much for him as for myself. I strode out of the car on to the sidewalk. Brandon opened the trunk and reached in and took out my packages. "I'll help you bring them up to your apartment."

"Good. Then you can eat some of Lapita's homemade tamales and enchiladas. It's lunch time."

"Again I can't do that," he said entering the lobby. When we turned and made a quick right to the elevators, getting off the elevator, Robert passed us. This time with a blonde. I glanced up at him and he threw me a sexy smile and nodded at me, teasing me. Brandon and I walked to the penthouse elevator. When the door closed, Brandon said, I think he likes you, Mrs. Blackstone."

Chapter 6

"That is putting it mildly," I said, my eyes looking up, my teeth tightening.

"Yes, I know. I can't say what I want out of respect for you," Brandon said to me. "You need to watch that man since your husband is not around. But if you need me, call anytime."

"I will, Brandon. Thanks." He laid my packages in the living area and stood and passed his hands through his blond hair.

"Wow. That is a sight, Mrs. Blackstone."

"I said the same thing myself when I first saw Central Park from here." I smiled, stood, and looked out.

"I mean this apartment with this view. Mr. Blackstone must love you."

"Yes, I guess he does…" And my little dog came running. I knew what time it was. "He bought me this dog to keep me company. I must walk him." He jumped into my arms. I grabbed the leash and headed out of the apartment with Brandon on the side of me petting my little dog. When the elevator reached the lobby we strolled outdoors.

"I'll park the car in the garage," he said.

"Here's the code. I'll wait for you." It didn't take Brandon but a few minutes. Just enough time for the dog to do his business, and Brandon was back handing me the keys. He unhitched his bike and rode away.

I strolled along thinking about Max. Looking down at the puppy, I spied a pair of eleven size perfect polished shoes, the kind I'd seen on Max. A pair of expensive Italian bespoke black leather shoes made especially for those feet. I raised my head staring, taking in a pair of long legs inside a pair of perfectly tailored black slacks and an alligator belt holding on to a white shirt that fit so well inside his pants. His waist small, his shoulders wide, his face strong, his smile perfect, and his blue eyes bright and carefree stopping me in my tracks and taking my breath away.

"Oh, you again," I said breathlessly, trying to affect a condescending tone. He reached out to pat my dog and I pulled it away. Poor dog, he didn't understand, he looked at me with his sad big eyes. "What do I have to do to get rid of you?" I said.

"Have dinner with me. In my apartment." The thought may have crossed my mind, but all I could visualize was my weakness for this stranger. I didn't know what I was capable of doing or what he was capable of doing to me.

"Do you think I would get close to your apartment? Who knows what goes on in there?"

"Are you jealous? Are you concerned with what I do in my apartment? It's probably more interesting than anything in yours." I raised my eyebrow and with a huff I turned to walk away. He stood in front of me, and said, "Then invite me to your apartment for dinner."

"That's like inviting Dracula in." He smiled and I put my dog down and hurried along back to the building with him walking beside me, and then he was ahead of me and made a sudden stop turning to face me.

"What if I invited you to a restaurant for dinner? Somewhere safe?" he said with a brazen smirk.

"I don't make dates with strange men when my husband is away."

"So, Blackstone is away. That means you will be calling me sooner than you think."

"That will be the day," I said, and I sauntered away from him, inside the lobby of my apartment building, hoping for protection from him, hoping for protection from my own sadistic and erotic thoughts of him. The doorman called out to me and jolted me back to reality.

"Mrs. Blackstone, a gentleman said that he was your brother-in-law and that I should let him go up to your apartment. He looked a hell of a lot like Mr. Blackstone, so I sent him up."

"That's fine, Ralph." My mind wasn't on Jonas, it was on the tall seductive stranger and when I looked around, he was standing behind me.

"Now I see I will have to navigate around two men to get to you? Here's my card. Call me if you need me," he said with a whisper, his inviting lips invading my mind when I stared at him. He handed me his card and for some reason I reached for it.

I glanced at the card. "A lawyer," I mumbled, my eyes blinking for a second. "Oh God, another one," I closed my eyes murmuring, "That's all I need." He looked my way, and I tossed it in the nearest trash bin.

⸻ ◈ ⸻

WHEN I ARRIVED IN THE safety of my apartment, I dropped the dog off near his bed, and he scampered to his nearest resting spot—under the couch. No one was home, which was good because I wanted to talk to Jonas and get him out as soon as possible and let him get back to Crystal. I didn't need him around with his shallow thoughtless behavior.

"Jonas," I said, calling out to him. He stepped from the dining table and headed in my direction.

"Alex. You are more beautiful than the day I first met you. Having a baby does wonders for you. He kissed me on both cheeks, then gave me a hug that lasted a few minutes. That hug worried me, but then everything about Jonas made my skin crawl. I looked into his dark eyes.

He fell on my sofa with a large sigh. "What's wrong now, Jonas?" I sat pensively gazing at him and his theatrics when he balled his fist and put it to his mouth. Then with his fist he tapped his forehead over and over until I took his hand and held it.

"Well. Well," he said exhaling, and lowering his head.

"Get to the point," I said, knowing he would tell me anyway. But with him, it would take a lot longer with a few dramatic effects thrown in for good measure. I didn't have time for him. I lost enough time with him in San Francisco. The stress of him in jail and Jonas and Max accused of murdering his fiancée. Too much drama came with Jonas.

"You know how Max said that he wouldn't help me again if I got in trouble."

"Don't tell me... you did something stupid again?" He nodded his head like a child who was caught pinching his little brother.

"Don't judge me, Alex. But... but I'm in trouble. It has to do with one of my BDSM clubs in Manhattan. It wasn't me this time." He raised both hands. "One of my patrons went too far with one of the girls and she..."

"Did she die?"

"No. But she was in bad shape and she threatened to call the cops. And she wanted a large settlement to keep it quiet. I was low on money because of Crystal, and my businesses..."

"Never mind Crystal, and never mind your business. What happened?" I said to him, pissed beyond belief. I never liked to waste time with all the intimations and ceremonies Jonas would take me through, because after all, we would end up at the same place, and my way we would get to the point sooner.

"There is this lawyer, and he did me a favor by taking care of the situation. When I asked him what he wanted in return, he said... I know this is crazy." I sat waiting for the crazy part that always accompany Jonas. "He said, he wanted my brother's wife for a night."

"He said what?" I cocked my head to the side, trying to wrap my mind around that statement. I sat up straight, stunned. "And what did you say?"

"I said of course not. I was right to say that wasn't I, Alex?" And his eyes grew large and sad.

"What the fuck do you think, Jonas?"

Jonas moved close to me and touched my hand and I stood up and pointed. "Get out."

"You don't know Alex, it's more than that. If you don't do this, my life is over. Crystal will leave me, Max will turn his back on me, and my partners will kill me," he said matter-of-factly. No emotion, no tears. His face cold, pale, and lifeless.

"I'm begging you, Alex." Jonas shamelessly got on his knees. "It's not like you haven't done this before."

"What am I expected to do?" I hissed, my voice unsympathetic and quiet. "And for how long?" My voice cracking. My eyes could have burned through Jonas. Here I was mixed up with his weird bullshit again. *Why me?* I asked the heavens.

"The lawyer wants you as his Domme."

"As his *what!* Have you lost your mind? Don't answer that. I know you have a few issues, to be exact, you have a lot of issues." I sat down and leaned back in my chair trying to recover, my hand clutching my mouth. I stood up and paced around the room, then coming back to Jonas, I said, "That doesn't sound like a temporary thing. And how am I to keep that from Max. If he found out something like that, we would both be pariahs in his eyes. He would take my boys."

"I won't let that happen."

"How could you stop it?" I questioned.

"The lawyer is a decent enough guy. He just likes to be flogged. That's all you have to do. He won't see you because he wears this hood over his head. He doesn't want to be recognized. Just one hour, you cane him, and then it's over. I'm going to monitor everything." Jonas's begging eyes glanced at me knowing that I wouldn't let him get killed over something as simple as flogging a man.

"Who knows, Alex, you might enjoy taking your frustrations out. It can only be good for your relationship with Max."

"Shut up." I narrowed my eyes. "If you say one more word..." I thought of something. "Maybe we can pay him off. I have loads of money Max put in my account. And then there's the money my birth mother left me in her will."

"That's no good. I think he has more money than he knows what to do with. It's not money he's looking for, Alex." I tried every way possible to get out of this quagmire Jonas just threw me in. "When is Max due to return? Jonas asked."

"Tomorrow," I said, hoping he would call it off.

"What. Why so soon?" Jonas said standing, and walking in a circle threading his hands through his dark hair.

"Max tries to be home on Saturdays. Could you have done more to fuck up my life?" Jonas walked to his leather bag and pulled out a slick black short dress.

"What's with the bag and that dress?"

He took a minute responding as if he was searching for a lie. "You will have to wear this." I gazed at him. He knew by my scorching glare that if I had a weapon, I would probably kill him, so he dropped the obscene black cat suit on the chair near me. "I brought it from my shop. It's all the rage," he said, pointing at the short black leather dress. It's one of my best sellers on play night. "Good thing you didn't pick up any weight when you had the baby. It's a size six."

"Am I supposed to feel better?" I said wrinkling my nose and glaring at the dress. "How am I to get into your place without anyone seeing me?"

"I run a high-class joint with high-class clientele."

"Sure you do, Jonas Blackstone. You are the same Jonas who married a teenager and her parents blackmailed you, and Max had to pay them off. This is just another one of your schemes that will probably go south, leaving me holding the bag like you've done so many times to Max."

"Not this time. I have lots of respect for you, Alex. And I have Crystal to keep me in check."

"Stop the bullshit, Jonas. Remember me, we both had a fucked-up childhood. I'm trying to straighten mine out, and here you are getting ready to..."

"I wouldn't ask you, but Crystal is pregnant and the baby needs a father."

"Just like my sons need their mother. Remember?" I peeked at Jonas with his head down and I felt sorry for him. Maybe that was what Max was trying to tell me. Jonas couldn't help fucking up his life and those that came around him. He didn't mean any harm. He just wasn't right when he came home from Afghanistan. "Just this once," I said, pointing a finger at him. I gave in against my better judgment.

He took my hand and kissed it. I looked at him and shook my head. "Can my driver take me there and wait for me?"

"No, Alex. You have to be discreet. Take a cab. I'll make sure you have transportation back." I shot a worried glance at him. "And wear one of your wigs and carry your silk black mask," he said.

"Anything else?" I said in my most sarcastic voice. "This had better be the truth."

"I swear," Jonas said, holding up two fingers."

Chapter 7

I couldn't sleep at all for wondering what could go wrong. I had to look at the costume that Jonas had given me. I tried it on. It fitted great. Maybe I could wear it when Max came home. *What am I doing with this?* I let out an emotional breath. I knew my husband wanted this from me, and yet I denied him. Now I'd agreed to pleasure another man.

I held a cup of coffee to my lips when Jonas walked out of the spare bedroom into the dining area, dressed in black slacks and white shirt with a black trim on the collar, looking as handsome as Max, and after all, they were twins I had to remind myself. He strolled in relaxed, headed over to the warmer, and dished out his breakfast.

He held a plate containing sausage and scrambled eggs. He picked up two toasted English muffins, dropped them on his plate, and sat across from me. "Hand me the strawberry preserves, will you, Alex?"

"For a second, I thought you were Max, but I remembered that tattoo on your hand. It took me a while to realize there were two of you. Twins and different as night and day."

"Not in the looks department..." he said, sipping his coffee and giving me a closed smile, "...and not what we expect from women."

"Let's not discuss that, we're getting into yucky territory," I said. "What time will I have to be at your place? And how long will this last?" Jonas placed a forkful of eggs into his mouth, and drank his orange juice, after drinking a cup of black coffee.

"An hour," he said between chewing his food.

"An hour?" I questioned, choking on a small sip of orange juice.

"I must charge by the hour, even if you're not expected to be there that long. The price for a good Domme with all these rich bastards who want discretion and want to remain anonymous is one hundred thousand an hour. A good sub is fifty."

"What are you doing with the money?" I narrowed my eyes. He must be making a fortune. Jonas turned with his eyes clouded. His mind lost somewhere.

"I had to pay the middlemen. In New York, you have to do these things," he said, raising his hands in desperation. "Everyone gets a piece of the pie. It's a part of doing business in this town." Jonas sauntered to the window, glaring at the Manhattan skyline.

"Then why don't you go back to San Francisco?"

"All the excitement is here, and all the money is with these billionaires. Max has the best Domme in all the world, and that's you, Alex." Jonas's eyes widened like a crazed man and then faded to me. When his green eyes met mine, they darkened. "He doesn't know how lucky he is. He has the most sought-after woman in this world of bondage, and some men would do anything for a woman like you."

I couldn't believe Jonas. He had lost what little mind he had left. My hands tightened on the chair. He had just parted with information I was sure Max didn't want me to know about, nor did I care to hear about my going price in the world of Bondage.

"This is the first and last time. You just tell that lawyer that I'm no one's mistress. Does he know that Max is my husband?"

"No. I'm not that stupid." I rolled my eyes at him. I just said that I knew someone from San Francisco that serviced Maximillian Blackstone. He doesn't know anything about you and Max."

"You're using Max as a poster boy for BDSM?" I closed my eyes in disbelief. "Jonas, get the hell out of here."

Jonas drank a glass of water, said goodbye to the dog after giving him a treat, and trotted out the door. I hoped he wasn't desperate enough to do something completely dangerous, but then he was Jonas Blackstone, the most carefree, callous, sexually uninhibited, handsome man I knew—my brother-in-law, and he scared the hell out of me.

MY NERVES HAD GOTTEN the best of me after talking to Jonas. I told Lapita to take care of the children and the dog, because I felt sick to my stomach. She took them to the first floor where their playroom was located. My plans were a long shower to wash away how dirty I felt with Jonas. Afterwards, I lay down across my bed and stared up at the lights in the chandelier until it hypnotized me into a long sleep and into thinking I could do this.

Still not convinced after I woke that I could pull this off, but I had to because I promised Jonas. I dressed about 6 p.m. I packed the Catwoman costume in my thirty-thousand-dollar insane designer bag. I placed the cat-o-nine tails I had used on Max, and I brought along handcuffs, and a black silk mask the kind you would wear to a costume ball. I wasn't taking any chances with that man seeing me or getting near me. I had to remember to get in there and beat him to submission and get out without anyone being the wiser. *That should be easy,* I thought.

Now all I had to do was get through my lobby without that devilishly handsome man seeing me. It was as if he timed me, or had cameras around, why else would he show up as often. I'd lived in here for a year, and never had the same hours as anyone else.

I made it off the elevator and into the lobby. I asked the doorman to call a cab. There was one waiting nearby and he flagged him down. I took a deep breath. *So far, so good,* I thought. I checked my pulse because it was beating so fast. I exhaled. Just as I was climbing into the yellow cab, I turned to make sure no one saw me, and our eyes met. He hurried to the door and was out standing near the cab before it took off, rushing to the window, then leaning in, he said, "Do you need a ride?"

"Do I look like I need a ride? Please, leave me alone."

"You smell delicious." And he passed his tongue over his top lip. Nervously fidgeting with the buttons, I managed to raise the window.

"Cabby, please leave." Robert stepped away and the cab pulled from the curb. I didn't look back because I was so anxious. I thought I would faint. *What am I doing?* dashed through my mind. "It's for a good cause, it's for a good cause, and I'm saving Jonas's life," I mumbled over and over, rocking in the back seat of the cab.

—⊙—

I ARRIVED AT A BEAUTIFUL stately mansion, hidden away behind shrubbery and trees, which probably belonged to some newspaper baron in the eighteenth or nineteenth century. It stood in the middle of Park Avenue near Fifth. The mansion appeared inconspicuous, and like most of the stately homes of years gone by, a façade of gargoyles could be seen perched near the windows. There was nothing that screamed there were unsavory acts going on behind its walls. The house was well maintained. It took money to renovate something of that magnitude and Jonas was overreaching. He was in so high up over his head that it would be a disaster if he came down to earth.

Jonas was no different from most siblings. They had to prove to someone that they were successful too. After feeling like a failure his whole life, Jonas struck out on his own to prove to Max that he could be as successful as Max, but Jonas was never a businessman. He had too many distractions, and now he was adding one more distraction to his collection—Crystal and a baby.

Now I was becoming part of the deceptions that Jonas was known for. But who could resist that beautiful, innocent, troubled man-boy? After all he was Max's brother. I guessed I could do this one favor for him, this one time. I looked around, he had to have sunk lots of money into this venture, and I prayed it worked for him. I paid the cabby, and the glare I received from his eyes when he handed me my change, told me he knew what was going on behind those stately doors.

I reached into the pockets of my trench coat and fished out the card Jonas gave me. I pulled down the tight black Catwoman suit. In my bag I had a special whip made for me by Max. I felt guilty using it, but I had more and I would throw it away. Get rid of the evidence so to speak. I felt like I was committing a crime and I had to get rid of the body.

The red wig I was wearing, after I got a distance from Robert, I pulled it over my hair before I reached this destination. I was dying to wear the wig for Max, and somewhere deep inside, I felt a tinge of excitement run through me.

My life had been so boring lately. Wasn't it meant to be that way since my husband was gone all the time, and I had two young children? I scolded myself. Did I agree to this madness because of Jonas, or to alleviate my bored existence and satisfy an urge? As I neared the door and pushed the bell, I thought, *Oh my god, I need a hobby.* I sucked in a full breath and an empty smile slid over my face.

The small window opened and a pair of dark brown eyes peered at me. I opened the trench coat showing the sleek black short leather dress, six-inch black patent leather heels, and then I placed the black and gold card in front of my face. The large mahogany door swung open. The mansion's foyer was dark, except for dimly lit sconces hanging along the wall in the shape of small chandeliers, which did nothing to brighten the place.

I kept walking behind a tall elegantly dressed man in a black suit. He said to follow him to the desk. An attractive blonde with dark eyebrows greeted me, giving away that she was anything but a natural blonde, but who was these days? I smiled at her and she smiled warmly back, and said, "This way."

"We were waiting for your arrival," she said, turning to glance at me and then she continued walking.

"Who's we," I said to her.

"Jonas... I mean Mr. Rich said that he was expecting you. The card you presented was one of his. He only gives them out to our specialists—the men and women who have achieved the status of Master or Mistress in this sexual art of pleasure." I glanced at her and noticed that she had been thoroughly indoctrinated by Jonas. He had that way of convincing young women who had just arrive here from a small city or farm, that he was some kind of Svengali, and would act as their protector and mentor.

If I didn't know him and I had laid eyes on his beautiful face for the first time, I probably would have fallen prey to his soft-spoken voice and innocent eyes, but I fell for the twin with the brooding, stoic, and pensive disposition hiding behind a beautiful handsome face, and a body that would send me on all fours and begging for more.

"I'm an artist?" I asked, not believing what I heard coming from the young woman who was all of twenty and not a day more.

"Of course you are. Art is not just for poets, writers, actors, and painters," she said, her head bobbing side to side as she spoke. "All individuals who achieve at the highest level in their field are considered artists," she continued, raising her head and eyeing me.

"And what is your area of expertise?" I asked her.

"I'm still a novice, but the Master says that I will be the best sub money can buy. He's grooming me and he's my mentor. I'm still at the proficient stage, until Jonas, I mean Mr. Rich gives me the okay. Now I only service him." Now I knew why Crystal was upset.

"I see. And what else does the Master say?" I questioned raising an eyebrow.

"He says that securing a Domme like you wasn't easy, and that you command a fee of one hundred thousand or more just for one hour." She paused, looking at me, "Whenever he can bring an artist of your standing into our establishment, word gets around, and our rooms are booked every day for the entire year. We have large crowds at our play nights, where Doms and subs demonstrate their expertise. It would be fun to have you join us one night."

I bet it would, I thought. "That will be the day," I quietly murmured.

The sub stopped and pointed to the door. "The Master's office. I'm not allowed in there."

After a long dark walk through an unending corridor of doors, I made it into Jonas's office. He stood with a pleasant smile, then strutted from behind his wide mahogany desk to greet me, and gave me a hug. His office was bright and cheerful, unlike the hallway leading there. Tiffany lamps everywhere. His smile was one of relief.

"I thought you weren't coming," he said, exhaling and grabbing me and embracing me tight, his nose touching my neck. "You smell great." I pulled away from him.

"You didn't tell me you were charging more than one hundred thousand dollars."

"I said that a Domme can command one hundred K. I have to charge that, and then there are the extras. I owe that to that fucking lawyer," he said, walking behind his desk and sitting in his dark leather chair, then placing his legs leisurely on his desk. I got a look at his Italian bespoke shoes, the kind Max wore.

"Enough of your crying, Jonas. Show me to the room and let's get this over with. I have children, a husband, and a puppy that thinks I'm his mother. I don't need any more complications in my life," I said, pulling out the whip and striking it on his leather chair. My eyes were a fiery glow. Jonas jumped at the sound and stood.

"Alex. Alex. Alex."

"What?" I said, turning around.

"Nothing." Jonas saw that I was angry and who wouldn't be angry? I couldn't believe I'd let him talk me into this irrational idiocy.

"The client is waiting," he said, ushering me to the door.

"Is he bound and gagged and does he have his mask over his head where he can't see me?" Knowing Jonas you should ask specific questions. I looked at him. "Well?"

"Well, not quite," he said, threading his hands through his dark curly hair. "He said he would pay an extra fifty thousand if you would handcuff him."

"I'm not going in there," I said.

"But you must, Alex. I oversold the fantasy. I promised him that he would never have a mind-blowing experience such as the one you will provide, and he will never forget it in a lifetime."

Chapter 8

"What?" I said blinking my eyes, and seething with anger. It was at that moment I had been angry enough to strangle Jonas with his own belt.

"I was just paraphrasing Max's words when he first met you, and you did what it is you do."

"But that was for Max to enjoy. Only Max. I didn't know what I was doing, then. I read a few articles and the rest I googled, then I tried it on Max. I was in love with Max. And Max loved me. It was more of what his mind told him."

"Pretend he's Max."

"I can't believe you. How in the hell am I going to do that?" I headed for the door. Jonas ran after me and stood in front of me.

"Please, Alex. Just do it once and I'll be out of debt, and I'll never bother you again. Do this for Crystal and the baby."

Shaking my head, my eyes blinking, I said to him, "Show me the room." He walked behind me, measuring his distance down the corridor. The walls were soundproof. Great. The lights dim. Great. You couldn't hear the screams and lashes and who knew what else going on inside the rooms, and I'd bet it was a lot. Jonas spent a pretty penny and probably Max's money to equip the mansion with exotic beds and furnishings which hid what was really going on behind closed doors.

"By the way, you look gorgeous and you look the part. That wig could fool Max." My eyes shot to him and he shut up.

"Get out!" I had to calm myself before I walked out of the door behind him. I looked over and there was a bar and some snacks. A menu was sitting nearby. I looked at it. No wonder he was in debt. He was offering too many amenities. Breakfast, dinner and supper, champagne, and caviar. Maybe I was missing something. *Who stays from breakfast through dinner?* Nothing but a sex addict with too much money and too much time.

I tried not to think about Max. When I became his Domme slash sub, he was riding me night and day and then falling asleep, then was ready to go again, when he wasn't flying around the world. Now it was different and nothing was the same between us.

I poured brandy in a snifter, and I knew you were supposed to sip it, but I drank it down in one gulp. I looked at my expensive watch, a present from Max, and placed it in my bag and deposited my expensive bag in one of the drawers. The client was late. *Jonas said he was here. Why do I fall for Jonas's lies?* I raised my head to the heavens praying for a miracle. Then the door opened and I turned around. Could anything get worse? There standing in front of me was that lawyer, Robert, from my apartment building.

I checked my mask to make sure it was on tight, and I saw that he wasn't wearing one as Jonas had said.

I guessed he was on vacation and he was making the best of it. I tried to steady my hands and calm my heart. I had to appear as if I knew what I was doing. I was breathing hard because I needed to get this over with.

When I gained control of my voice because the drink was working, I said, "You asked for a Domme? I'm here and you're late."

He smiled that beautiful mischievous smile, "I guess you will have to punish me hard," he said.

"Don't smile at me. Don't look at me, and don't touch me. Take everything off except your boxers."

He had on slippers and a robe that were provided by the establishment. "I don't wear boxers, I have nothing on under this," he said, opening the robe.

"This is irregular and against the rules. You should have your boxers under that robe."

"I don't wear any. Ever."

That explains some things.

He slid the robe off quickly as if he had practiced that maneuver a hundred times. And watching all the women coming and going with him, he was an expert. He was an artist. I thought he liked showing off his firm beautiful hard body. I stood watching him mesmerized at his wide chest and small waist.

"Then put on…" His eyes locked on me watching his hard penis. I had to say to myself, *"Get a hold on yourself. This will be over soon. I know you are hot, but don't cross that line. Even if you want him to fuck you and eat you, don't let him do it."*

He stood before me showing a hard hairless chest with a six pack to die for. His muscles were firm, his arms like rocks. I was the one being seduced by that handsome man and he knew it. This would make for an interesting night. "Weren't you supposed to wear something over your head, and I agreed to this because I was assured that you would follow the rules," I said, stepping closer to the door.

"Rules are made to be broken," he said, shooting me a wicked smile, his eyebrow raised reminding me of Max.

"I took precautions and I wore my mask."

"I didn't follow your orders on purpose. Now I know you must beat me. I have disobeyed all your orders." He turned with his hard butt. I reached for a cat-o-nine tails and drug it lightly over his butt until I saw chills form. Then I hit him with all my might. *Whack! Whack! Whack!* "Is that all you have?"

He leaned against the bedpost and I hit him again, and this time, I took out the handcuffs which I had near just in case he tried anything. I reached for his hands and he volunteered them. I put them on quickly behind his back.

I walked to the tall closet and reached in and brought out a cane. I showed it to him.

I got a reaction out of him I didn't expect. "Beat me. I deserve it. Beat me." After I thought I had done enough to his beautiful back and butt, I released the handcuffs and threw them on the bed.

He fell on all fours, and I placed a collar around his neck with straps, and I hopped on his back, and he made a noise as if he was a horse, and looking at the size of his dick the horse had nothing on him. He scurried around the room bucking me and I felt the tingling of my clit on his bare back. When I felt something I wanted to punish him more. I hit him relentlessly on his butt with a belt.

When he couldn't walk on all fours anymore, I climbed off, and he fell to the side of the bed and lay in a fetal position. I knew what he wanted, I had to place the handcuffs on him. I cuffed his hands behind his back and stood over him. He began sniffing me. I pulled the chain around his neck to restrain him. When I kneeled near him to place the black silk tie over his eyes, he licked my thigh.

"Stop!"

"Then whip me," he said, "I'm your dog, I'm your slave now and forever." Turning his head looking at me, before I could reach my whip, he used his teeth to rip my thong off and he pushed me down lying over me. Holding me down with his hands cuffed, he managed to sniff my legs, he raised my dress with his teeth and his tongue trailed from my belly button to my opening, as I struggled and fought to get him off me.

With his hands busy holding me, he used his head to open my legs wide. He felt them trembling. "Calm down. Let me do this. You will not be disappointed." I pushed him away, but he held me down and eased his mouth over my mound with a burst of satisfied moans.

The heat coursed through me and every part of me lit up. My nipples were hard, my clit was hard, and when he placed his tongue on my clit it quivered. He looked up at me and smiled.

I don't know what he did, but his tongue slowly found my bud and then I lay there seduced by how enjoyable the experience had become.

I forgot who I was in this room where no one but us would know what went on that day. I gave in to his wonderful tongue and hard body. I gave in to the orgasmic rush that came pouring from my body.

I snapped back to reality. I'd had an orgasm with another man, and it wasn't Max.

I reached for the belt and I hit him over and over and there he lay begging for more. He pulled himself up and placed his back against a chair in a seated position, and he said, "I have to have you again." I looked at him. All those women going to his apartment and he was asking to see me again.

"This is not going to happen again. Ever," I said to him.

"I need to see you." He stood satisfied and walked to the restroom. I reached for my purse in the drawer. I saw him take the latex off that beautiful hard dick and throw it in the basket and I threw my torn undies in my purse, grabbed my trench coat, and rushed through the door.

I slipped out of the room with my dignity in pieces. At least it didn't go any further than him putting his tongue in me, but this was never supposed to happen. I didn't wait to talk to Jonas. I ran down the hall and rushed to the front door. The guard opened it for me and I stood outside panting and looking around. No cab. "Oh shit, I forgot Max's belt." I sure as hell wasn't going back. Reaching inside my bag, I found my phone.

"Hello, Brandon?"

"Mrs. Blackstone?"

"Yes. It's me."

"You sound strange. What do you need?" Brandon said.

"Can you pick me up at 580 Park Ave.?"

"You know, Mrs. Black…"

"Call me Alex."

"Yes, I can pick you up, but all I have is a motorcycle."

"I don't care. How long will it take?"

"Maybe ten minutes."

"That's find come now."

I trudged down Park Avenue waiting for Brandon when a limo cruised by. Most limos appear to be the same, however, I had a thing about numbers, and from Max driving and parking and stalking me in Seattle, I became nervous thinking that Max had found out about my indiscretions. Not only the one I'd just perpetrated, but the secret that I hid in my heart and body and soul—that I was attracted to another man just like Max.

I peeped around the corner to see where the limo was going. It was the very place I had escaped from. Imagine me running into Max. My imagination and conscience had gotten the best of me. I looked and there was Brandon driving his motorcycle at breakneck speed, zooming in and out of traffic.

"What the hell am I doing here?" I murmured. I tried my best to look inconspicuous, but the flaming red wig and six-inch heels wasn't helping my case.

Brandon's motorcycle slid to a stop and he angled it to the curb where I could easily jump on. "Mrs. Blackstone?"

"It's me, Brandon. Don't ask." I pulled the wig off, climbed on behind him, put my hands around his waist, laid my head on his shoulders, and said, "How did you get here so soon?"

"When you called I was at a friend's house."

"Can you take me where I can get a drink and comb my hair?"

"I know a local tavern. Hang on." He started the bike and we went charging through the streets. He did try to drive a bit slower than before, but his feet were heavy. The ride was exhilarating, nonetheless. It gave me time to clear my head and wonder what Max was doing because I knew what I had just done.

We came to a sudden stop at a neighborhood bar close to my apartment, but not too close. Brandon helped me off the bike. Glancing at me, he appeared confused, but he said, "It's none of my business and I won't ask you about your business, but why didn't you call me. I would have taken you there and waited for you."

"It's not that easy and I can't explain. Please, don't ask me any more questions. I'm not feeling too good now." I tottered into the bar holding on to Brandon. We sat at a table and I ordered a beer and Brandon ordered the same. When it arrived, I guzzled it, placed it on the table and rushed to the ladies' room. I combed my hair, turned, and kicked the six-inch shoes to the side, wiped my face clean, and looked in the mirror amid the curious stares of two young women. "I like your shoes," one girl said, dressed in a short black leather skirt."

"You can have them."

She picked them up and examined the red soles, "They're Christian Louboutin. Are you're sure?" she said.

"Do you want them?"

"Sure," she said. "Thanks." She looked to her friend and gave her the thumbs up. And she walked out with them. I tossed on a pair of ballet slip-ons from my purse. I glanced at myself, then I pulled my hair up into a ponytail, wiped the red lipstick off and took a good look in the mirror. "Yes, me again," I said. A youthful brunette of twenty-four, with children, married to a fucked-up sex addict, love of my life, the handsome, rich, desirable, Maximillian Blackstone.

I tightened the belt on the trench. "Now get your ass home before you regret this," I murmured.

The words fucked-up sex addict echoed in my brain as the door closed behind me. I walked over to Brandon, "Take me home now." He paid the check, opened the door, and helped me on to the motorcycle and we took off. "Drop me off a half a block from my home," I yelled when he slowed near my apartment.

I made it home at ten o'clock. Brandon, my lifeline, saved my life. "I need you to be on call. I'll pay you a bonus."

"Whatever, Mrs. Blackstone. If you need me for any reason just call." I thanked Brandon, gave him a kiss on the cheek, which surprised and embarrassed him. He had been there for me, and I wouldn't forget it. I waved goodbye to him. I walked the next block home and rush through the doors of my apartment building. "Safe," I murmured.

I wobbled to the desk, and asked the doorman, "Have you seen Mr. Blackstone come in this evening?"

"No, Mrs. Blackstone. I haven't seen him. I just got on this shift." I smiled and headed for the penthouse elevator, praying that I didn't run into anyone, especially that handsome man who could ruin my life any minute.

Breathing a sigh of relief, the elevator door opened into my penthouse lobby. Everyone had gone to bed. The children were sleeping in their rooms when I checked, and the dog slept curled up on Maxim's bed. I guessed the puppy found them after being deserted by me. Because he was still a baby, I didn't need him waking me up after this exhausting night. I needed me time and to figure out just what was happening in my life.

After taking a shower, I expected a call from Max, or at least he would show his face soon. I became worried. I remembered when he behaved like this once before when I was pretending to be someone else—a blonde Dominant. He became infatuated with the other me, because the other me gave him what he needed, a good flogging and every part of my body. He forgot the outside world and would spend nights at my apartment engaging in illicit sexual acts, which was great at the time because we loved each other, and we couldn't stay away from each other.

I began to worry. However, I knew the depths of his love for me and his boys, and he would be home, but just to make sure, I'd call Jonas to check.

"Jonas."

"Yes, Alex. You know I can't thank you enough. My client..."

"I didn't call to discuss your client. I called to find out if Max has been there tonight."

"Why, Alex? Why do you ask?"

"Don't do this, Jonas. Answer the fucking question."

"No need for hostilities after our partnership."

"What partnership?"

"The one we have."

"We have none. Now answer the question."

"No, Alex, I haven't seen Max."

"Can I talk to you tomorrow when you have rested and are not so...?" Jonas searched for the right word, "...not so hostile."

"No!" And I pushed the button, laid the phone on a nightstand, and went to bed. I began to doubt my eyes and my senses. I'd get some sleep and call Max in the morning. I was too tired now and I needed some distance between me and Jonas's craziness.

Chapter 9

I woke and ate a small breakfast. "Where is everyone?" I wondered. Picking up the iPhone I decided to text Max. It shouldn't be too much to expect a text back, something from his secretary. It wasn't like him to do this now. But he had done this before, that was before we were married, even then he would at least spend the night with me, even if he disappeared in the morning.

Finally, I understood what was happening, he would get Jonas out of one fix after another. Now Jonas has ensnared me into his web of deceit, where he was the only one who came out on top.

Today was our day, mine, and Max's, where we could forget our troubles and have our date night without children, animals, nannies, and noise. We would just lie back and engage in the bases of sexual deviancy we could create for each other. After last night, I was looking forward to the peace and quiet of being tied up, and letting him have his way with me. Maybe I could get out of my head the visions of Robert naked.

I reached for my phone and called Brandon. "Brandon, pick me up in front of my building at seven tonight. Get the midnight-blue Bentley at six thirty. I need you to drop me off at 455 Park Avenue. I'll remain at that address until the next day."

"Anything else you would like me to do, Mrs... I mean, Alex?"

"Go back to my garage when you have dropped me off and park the car. Then get the car the next day about 9 a.m. And return to the same address and I'll wait for you in the lobby."

"I'll be there," Brandon said without questions. I was sure he was beginning to think all kind of unsavory thoughts about me. I couldn't blame him, because I had a few that were running around and tormenting me as well.

————◦————

I TRIED CALLING MAX again. He had his phone off. That was unusual. He knew never to turn his phone off. Because of the boys, he had to be available in case something happened. As I struggled to dress for my big night, I heard a knock at my bedroom door.

"Mr. Blackstone called last night," Lapita said, walking into the room without waiting for me to tell her to enter.

"What did he say?" I dropped the dress once I heard his name. I was nervous, wondering whether he found out about my affair, not an affair, no, it bordered more on betrayal.

"He said that he tried calling you, Miss, but you had your phone off and no one picked up on the house phone. He asked if everything was okay. I said it was and he hung up."

"Did he say anymore?"

"Only that he would see you at the other apartment, Miss." Lapita knew that we had an apartment not far from here, but what she didn't know was the salacious activities behind those doors. I could never tell her, because I didn't want to disturb her delicate sensibilities and have her raise an eyebrow at me whenever she looked at me or Max.

I don't think she thought there was life after children. I gave her the address and phone number just in case there were problems with the kids.

Watching the digital clock near my bed, made for a long and agonizing day. Anxious and excited to be with Max, I decided to go for a run in the park to limber up for my all-night sessions. I dressed in my running clothes, tied my hair in a ponytail, put on my running shoes and headed for the elevator. I made it to the lobby, made it through the lobby doors, and made it to the park without the embarrassment of seeing Robert.

I couldn't keep this up, dreading going downstairs in fear of running into that handsome man who now haunted me in my dreams. I had to admit to myself that I enjoyed every minute of what he did, and what I did to him. I could flog him again if I wasn't afraid it would cost me everything. The thought of punishing him and the enjoyment I garnered caused me to question my sanity. Since when did I enjoy this kind of thing? When I first met Max and understood what turned him on, my initial fear was that it would take over me, and it did. I just didn't think it would involve another man.

I had been out warming up and running for an hour when I heard a jogger slow down behind me. The person didn't want to pass me, which was clear enough. I slowed to almost a walk, breathing hard. Any man could pass me in a second. I continued running without looking around. If someone wanted to mug me it would have been stupid. The park was filled to capacity, large groups of people old and young were sitting around on the grass, eating snacks from vendors, and couples lounging on the benches with their dogs on leashes.

When I jogged further and I could see my building, I stopped to catch my breath, panting hard, bending down holding on to my knees. And the unknown person stopped. I could hear his sluggish breath and it wasn't because he wasn't in shape. I lifted my body and gradually turned to face the person behind me, standing so patiently, standing so close we could share the same space. I stared into his large blue eyes, his face expressive. I knew somehow before it was Robert. His body covered up with sweatpants and a pullover revealing taut muscles hiding under his shirt, which made him hot and me wanting him.

"Why are you following me?" I said comfortably and with courage, because my apartment was directly ahead, and all I had to do was cross at the light, and I was home. But women had been known to disappear in their front yards, but that was in suburbia, and usually it was the husbands who made them disappear.

Years of being with a man, having his children, having sex the way he wanted, didn't stop some men from doing away with their expendable wives. With all Max's money, he could make me disappear in a minute.

I kept thinking that maybe he found someone, and he was thinking about that person the way I thought about Robert. Maybe he wanted me to disappear.

I had to rein in my thoughts because they were drifting to infidelity and murder, and this wasn't Max. We hadn't reached that bridge yet. We were at another milestone. The rich happy beautiful couple, with the two beautiful children, and a dog, who had been married only a couple of years.

"I'm not following you, Alex," Robert said softly, too softly, his words mocking me and interrupting my thoughts.

"Don't call me Alex," I said in a huff. "Do you know who I am?" I said, raising an eyebrow to let him know I meant business. "I'm Mrs. Blackstone."

"And do you know who I am?" he countered with a soft smile.

"Yes, that asshole who shows up everywhere I go."

"I said I was on vacation. And if you don't mind, Mrs. Blackstone, I have a right to be here. Does your title deny me the right to this air? I don't think so." He made his point, and I recognized the truth. I twisted around and stood waiting for the light, and when it hit green, I jogged across the street. But I wasn't getting away from him just like that. He jogged with me and stood close behind me as the doorman opened the door.

I walked to the elevators which were side by side. I stood there hitting the button. It was the penthouse and I had to wait for it. I could feel his eyes on my body as he stood regarding me, making me nervous. I could have beat him. He was just the sort of arrogant good-looking fuck that begged for a good beating. I turned smiling, thinking of the possibilities.

"Why are you smiling at me?" Robert queried. "Keep it up, you look lovely when you smile. You need to smile more often."

"Because, you are going to get what you're looking for," I said with one brow lifted.

"Are you the one that will give it to me?" he said, leaning in with a smirk. He saw the look on my face. I blinked. I tried to present an expression as if he didn't matter. He was nothing to me. I even shot him a contrived smile, but he ignored me. He raised his head and sniffed. "Oh, that perfume. It smells..."

The elevator door finally opened. I rushed inside and he peeked his head in. "I've smelled that fragrance before. We all have our secrets. Now you know mine, and I know yours." And a smile took up all the space on his face. Even his eyes smiled wickedly.

"What are you talking about?" I said, startled and shaken.

"I like perfume on a woman and you like wearing it, Mrs. Blackstone," he said, stepping close to the elevator. I hit the button and it closed in his face. I could still see that sexy grin smeared on his handsome face.

I always wear my favorite perfume. Did I accidentally wear it that night? I didn't know it would be him waiting for me. I'm going to kill Jonas.

My nerves were rattled. Did he know it was me? "No." If that self-serving egomaniac knew, he would have shouted it to the world, or I would be a candidate for blackmail.

Feeling like a prisoner who had gotten a last-minute call from the governor, I let out a full breath and rushed inside the protected walls, and into my room to shower. I had a few minutes to get dressed and get to the apartment on time.

Rushing, I kissed my sons and said goodbye. When I reached the door, the doorman rang the buzzer informing me my chauffeur had arrived, and that he was waiting for me. I said to the doorman that I was on my way down. Because I didn't want to be late, I rushed in the elevator with my hair wet, and I wore the trench coat I had on at Jonas's place.

I stepped out of my private elevator the same time Robert stepped out of the elevator across from mine with one of his girls. He startled me and I dropped my purse, and all its contents scattered over the tile floor. I bent to pick up my lipstick, comb, and eyelash curler. I thought I had gathered everything from the floor, until, "Mrs. Blackstone, you forgot something."

Turning around he held out his hand, and in it, a black and gold card and a black thong balled tightly in his fist. It was Jonas's card and the thong he tore from my body when he licked me all over. "I think you'll need this." I reached for my thong, and he held it back. "Say please," he whispered stooping down meeting my eyes.

My eyes glaring into his gleaming blue eyes. "It's not what you think," I said.

"It's none of my business," he whispered, giving the thong to me, as he leaned into me. "We all have secrets, and I know yours." My eyes opened wide like saucers. The woman at his side looked on with jealousy brimming in her face. She didn't say a word. She waited as he smiled and touched my hand lightly. It looked like she knew what he was doing, and she couldn't stop him because she appeared to be his submissive.

It was clear now, those girls coming and going were subs.

As I pulled away from him, the notion struck me, she was his sub. Wasn't that ironic. She was his sub and I was his Domme. In that room he would do anything I wanted. The problem was he didn't know his place, or he'd disobeyed me on purpose. I could give him the things he needed—he desired and wanted to be punished by me.

We both possessed a morbid and dangerous fascination for each other.

I scowled at him, and whispered, "I know your secret and your weakness. You will never get a chance to feel that way again." I stood and strutted away. Brandon stood at the open door to my car, and I climbed in, and he closed the door. I pushed the button and the dark window slid down so I could get a better look at his face. I'd struck a blow, and I was enjoying the effects.

His gaze long and painful, remembering the exciting moments he had when he was with me. Realizing it may never happen again, I spotted that look on his face, pale and dark, eyes fixed as if in shock. It was the same look when I informed Max that I had planned to marry, and that I would no longer be his Domme.

I think that was why Max was so eager to marry me, that, and the children. What I gave him, he would never be able to replicate that with a wife or Domme. He had it all when he wanted it. And now I was bringing it to him and leaving this arrogant ass out in the cold to wander around and look for something that he would never get again. He would be trying his whole life to find someone to connect with him and provide his needs with understanding.

Looking at all the woman he had around him was an indication of what he was looking for and hadn't found.

"Mrs. Blackstone." Brandon shook me out of my thoughts. "Do you want me to wait for you?"

"No, that will not be necessary. You can drop me off and I'll contact you tomorrow."

"Are you going to be safe?"

"Perfectly safe. I'm having a date night with my husband."

"You rich people sure know how to live," Brandon said, smiling and shaking his head.

Chapter 10

Max had been trying his best to be the kind of man I wanted. He had been trying too hard. I couldn't believe that he would give up everything to make me happy. We moved back to New York where I could be comfortable. San Francisco, although a vibrant city, just wasn't for me. I needed more. Maybe I was just a thrill seeker in hiding. Now that I had met and tamed my Mr. Black, I was feeling as if there could be more. I didn't know why I felt that way. It was probably because my hormones had been raging since Jack was born.

I had everything I needed, and everything I've ever wanted, but something appeared to be missing in my life. This scenery was divine. I had a penthouse apartment overlooking Central Park, and all I could think about and wonder about was what was missing.

"I wonder where Max is," I voiced my concerns aloud. He usually called. The children were with the nanny at our other apartment and tonight was our night. But every time I made a date with him we had to reschedule. If things didn't get better, then I was going out and getting a job, or going back to school. I'd been threatening that a lot lately. More so to an empty room.

Max stated that he needed me here to take care of the children. I was there for the children, but I felt useless because of all the nannies he had hired against my wishes.

I opened the door to our apartment, dropped my trench coat and my eyes wandered, landing on the evening paper. I picked up the paper, sat in a chair, and read. This headline story is about a woman committing suicide. "Oh another story about a bored housewife," I murmured. She loved a man so much, but he deceived her with scores of women.

"Although she had beauty and money she didn't have the one thing her husband needed and wanted, and that was an heir." Turning away from the paper, I laughed. "I have that in spades. Two sons to carry on the Blackstone name. What else does he want?" I dropped the paper on the floor and when I turned, standing in the doorway, a brilliant set of green eyes hovered over me, and they were attached to Max. He reached and picked up the paper.

"I see you're catching up on your daily gossip." He smiled with his brilliant white teeth. He walked close to me, his nose trailing up and down my neck and then sniffing my hair. My skin reacted, bursting with chills. My opening heated and was ready to overflow.

He pulled me up into his arms, "You smell delicious. I could take you now on this chair." He kneeled in front of me and spread my legs with his hands.

"What are you doing? I know when you start our evening like this, you have to leave." He didn't answer me. His long lashes hid his fantastic green eyes, then he opened them wide with displeasure. He didn't want to have a conversation. He was like that. All his way or no way. He knew what I desired and that was any part of him. I could spend my whole life loving him if he wasn't so secretive. I thought when we married it would change with him, but it became worse.

He grabbed the strings of my black bikini and tore through the fine silk. The two-hundred-dollar underwear fell to the floor silently. The only sound came from me, and it was a whimper and moan.

Max kissed the inside of my thighs gently as he wrapped his hands round each leg. Kissing my inner thighs, he found my clit waiting for him, needing him. He stared at it and began to moan. Then he placed his fingers in my folds, and taking his fingers out, he placed them to his nose and into his mouth. "You have the same scent from the first time we met," he said, looking up from between my legs, his eyes sparkling with happiness and pleasure.

"That's because you have been neglecting your duties." As if he didn't hear me, he placed his head between my legs and his tongue found my clit. He swirled it around and I could feel his warm breath and his warm tongue enter me. I grew more excited and pulled my bra down, so he could reach my breasts without hindrance. My nipples jutted out, heated and elongated, and then his long arms found them like a ship finding a port that had been too long at sea.

He squeezed my nipples until they peaked and turned red. "I love you because you have a high tolerance for pain," he said.

"I hope it's more than that," I whispered.

"You are the most beautiful woman I've ever seen."

"More," I said.

"You are the mother of my sons."

"More."

"I love eating you."

"More."

"I love making love to you."

"More."

"Enough." Max seized my legs and pulled me to the floor. His eyes blazed, and he passed his tongue over his lower lip. He un-zipped his pants as he continued trailing his tongue around my clit, then sucked it hard.

"Give me what I want and what I need," he said. His voice broke with a husky whisper.

My legs were wrapped around his neck, he had my nipples in his hands, and his fingers were holding them like a vice, and I began to thrust my body into his face. In a minute he had me coming and I couldn't stop. I let out such a scream of satisfaction, then a moan from the satisfied release followed.

"Keep on. I want you like I have never wanted you before," he said, pulling off my robe, turning me over on my stomach, and gazing at my body with my bra now around my neck. He unhooked it and threw it to rest with my panties. He straddled me where I couldn't move, my face buried into the pillow, he leaned and reached for our supply of lubricants on the nearest table.

I had agreed to this apartment and keeping an ample supply of products to enhance our lovemaking. He was a man of strange tastes, and I knew it. I wanted to please him because he knew what to do to make me come on a dime. I had to be sure that he would want me as much as I needed him. I gave into him because we had the same crazy desires—kinky sex with each other.

His warm, nervous, and demanding hands spread my buttocks. He gazed at me as he put his thumb to his mouth and moistened it, before rimming it around my anus, sending chills through me. He gently placed his thumb in my anus spreading the cold lubricant, and with his other hand, he pried open my drenched opening as he ran his fingers around. Taking his thumb out, he placed a latex on his penis. He guided his full and heated penis into me.

I moaned with pleasure. He inched it in until I could feel the full length of him. Then he placed his hand under my belly and pulled my body up as I went on all fours. He began to kiss my back, gripping my hips as he made each hard thrust. His movements slow and unhurried as he crouched behind me, then he accelerated out of control. He pushed and pulled in and out of me, with me letting out a grunt, until he had his first orgasm, then another shortly afterwards. That was his way of preparing me for what I knew to be an endless night of kink.

I didn't mind because that was what he enjoyed above all else, but it had become our regular lovemaking. He would eat me, make me come, then he'd come inside my dark passage. We had been having anal sex more than vaginal sex. I began to wonder why.

I should have been happy that he desired me, knowing his dysfunctions with sex, but there was something missing. *Has the joy gone out for both of us, and it is just something we do out of convenience?* I wondered.

When he finished, he lay by the side of me. He was exhausted. I knew why with all the businesses that he promised to sell and for some reason he couldn't. He claimed it was because it was St. John who had tried to ruin him.

Just like the past, he made love to me, and then fell asleep. I had been his sleeping aid for more than two years since we were married. This apartment was our hideaway from the children, from the world. We could forget everyone and everything. After our orgies were over, then we would resume our regular husband-wife duties in our apartment across town.

Wasn't it wonderful to have this kind of arrangement? I couldn't answer that question now. But I was too young to leave alone with raging hormones, especially with a handsome man lurking around, and sending me flowers, wanting me to flog him, and who knew what else.

My indiscretions caused me to wonder about what other arrangements my Mr. Black might have. I wondered what he was doing when he left me to go around the world to sell his properties. I should have been happy, but I wasn't. There was something missing, and it was in me. After all, he agreed to sell everything because of me, and now I was having second thoughts. I couldn't stop thinking that I had betrayed him with another man and maybe he was doing the same thing to me with another woman.

⎯⎯⎯ ◉ ⎯⎯⎯

THE CLOCK STRUCK 5 a.m., and I reached over and found Max gone. I craved waking up and lying in his arms, now I felt like any warm body would do. He had made coffee and left me his usual notes. I couldn't stop him from writing those damn notes to me, especially since he'd rushed from the bed leaving me so early in the morning. I had been angry ever since I met him in Montana, and I requested no more notes.

Text me for God's sake.

I reached over and there it was. I decided to open it and read it. Usually I would ball it up and throw it into that gold-plated five-thousand-dollar basket. *"What are we doing with all that expensive shit?"* I asked myself? Too many homes, too many employees, and more clothes and shit than I would ever wear in a lifetime. I took a deep breath and began reading his note.

———⬤———

MY DARLING ALEX,

I have arranged for you to interview your driver. He will be yours exclusively to do as you wish. You don't have to wait on my driver because he will be tied up with me until I sell my hotels. I have a meeting this afternoon and I'll be late. If I'm too late, kiss the boys for me.

Love you,

Max

I explained to Max that I didn't need a driver. I could take a taxi if I needed to go anywhere. Now I had my driver and I forgot to pass it by him. I noticed that he didn't question me about anything lately. It would be nice if he asked about my day or the weather.

Once you got into the weather territory, you would know you had a problem with your marriage.

Chapter 11

Max I hated to leave Alex, but I was stressed over the selling of my Asian Properties. I promised her that I would be more attentive to her and the boys, but until I could get rid of my companies, I could never give her the attention she was expecting or requiring. I was sitting in my office gazing out of the window trying to figure something out. I hadn't picked up a contract or read anything lately.

"Hi, Max." It was Robert. "Why don't you accept my invitation and go to this bar with me today? You stay in this office all day when you're not in Hong Kong, then you rush out at night, and you're in at 6 a.m. When do you see your wife and when do you have a chance to enjoy yourself?"

He didn't realize that all I had was my wife and my sons. I didn't need anything or anyone. Since Alex came into my life she filled my every need. "I'm not leaving here until you agree to go with me tonight," Robert said standing facing me, and in front of the panoramic view he glanced over the city and turned with smile. I knew what he was thinking. I felt the same when I first bought this building near Wall Street.

I looked down and shuffled my papers on my desk pretending to be busy, hoping Robert would get the hint.

"It's Friday. I've got plenty of contracts to go through. I should read and sign these papers," I motioned to the stack on my desk. "I don't know. I promised Alex that I would get home early." I just told him a lie and I hoped he would stop pestering me. I couldn't afford to let him go, though. I depended on him because of my workload, and I felt I could trust him. Where was Jonas when I needed him? "Look, Robert, I'll let you know about eight." Another lie.

"You know I can stay if you want to be home with your family." I looked up and smiled. I knew he was trying to make my life a little easier. I guessed I must trust someone, but that wasn't my best suit, trusting outside people.

"I can take a few minutes. How about eight? I should be ready then."

I was hoping he'd say it was too late to go out. "Hell yeah, eight o'clock is good. This town doesn't start rocking until about eleven. Maybe we can have something to drink and eat first. Then we can get down to the business of having fun. You do know what fun is, don't you, Blackstone?"

He looked at me and I gave him a dry smile, lips closed. I was sure the word no was foreign to him. That was probably why I hired him. A persistent bastard. I remembered it was at Jonas's insistence. *Since when do I take Jonas's advice?*

"You must have taken the F out of fun, Blackstone, but I'm here to put it back," Robert said with a sly grin lighting up his eyes.

"Okay. Fine. Just get the fuck out of here and let me get some work done. Don't you have something to do?" I asked.

"Yeah. Yeah." And he backed out of the office, rubbing his hand on the Blackstone bust of my father sitting in the corner of my office.

I thought of my grandfather and how he had taken the name of Blackstone from a black rock used to sculpt famous figures. My grandfather had been an orphan from England and brought out west. It was there he made his fortune, and it was there my father died. I felt loneliness creep over me. All I had now was my sons, Alex, and my brother, Jonas.

Nothing mattered to me now. Not my money or land, only them.

I'd tried to be everything that Alex wanted. I knew she was everything I had hoped for. We had our sons, and I should be satisfied. I feared I was falling into my old ways. I needed to make an appointment to see my therapist. I couldn't concentrate on my work, and since Jonas had disappeared again, and Charles revealed that Jonas had been masquerading as me in my business meetings, I couldn't seem to get into the rhythm of my work. I didn't appreciate Jonas at the time. Now I wished he was around to help me and watch over my family.

Someone was knocking. "Max, I thought you would need a break. Let's get a drink and something to eat, it's lunch time."

Robert is relentless, pestering me trying to make friends. I was his employer not his friend. I hadn't had a friend since I was in grade school. I didn't need friends.

"You look like you could use a drink and a good fucking."

"Can we just talk about something else?"

"Whoa. Okay," he said, holding his hands up.

"I'll have one drink and then I'm going home. My wife and children are waiting for me."

I hated living in New York. I liked space and I liked to fish and ride my horses at my ranch in Montana, disappear into the woods, and camp for a week.

I glanced up at Robert, maybe I saw myself. I didn't have to say much, my face would say it all.

"The women like me," he said reading my expressive face, straightening his tie, and twisting his heavy watch around his arm. "The flasher the better. That shit you have on, all that black would attract only Dracula's bride." And he tugged at his collar. "The white shirt is okay, but lose the dark clothes."

"I didn't hire you as a clothing consultant. Besides, I'm your boss. I dress for success."

"Well, I dress for pussy. Had any lately?" I raised an eyebrow, and he knew he had stepped over the line. If I didn't need him, I would fire him immediately.

Talking to Robert was a waste of time. I needed some exercise and I agreed to leave the comforts of my building, walk down the street with this cock hound and stop in at a bar. I thought it would be one where you would find only men watching sports. I should have known.

We entered the stylish bar, with mirrors, mahogany wood, and women wall to wall gazing with dazzling smiles, and wearing tight low-cut dresses. We sat at a table and women passing on their way to the ladies' room would smile at him and drop their cards on the table. The waitresses wearing extremely short skirts knew him well, and I was sure in the biblical sense.

"See, Blackstone. The women love me. A man like you with his billions, and handsome, and not getting enough pussy from his wife, would be a god around here or anywhere."

"Well said for a single man, but ..."

"Yeah, Yeah. Save the shit for your wife," he said to me. I downed a Scotch over rocks and two more to calm me and keep me from firing him. After a few more drinks, and trying to keep my cool with Robert, I was disgustingly drunk. I talked too much about my life, and I knew it was time to go home.

"I'm leaving. My limo is waiting for me," I said to Robert.

"You look drunk as a skunk, two sheets to the wind. I'm riding with you. I can't drive." Robert was from Pennsylvania, he came back to New York after spending time in Texas. He came back and Jonas hired him. I could imagine where he met Jonas. Jonas was probably impersonating me in one of his BDSM clubs and using my money to support his habits.

We had been bar hopping around New York since one o'clock, and when I looked up it was 8 p.m.

Trying to make my way out of the crowded bar to my limo, Robert caught sight of me and ran after me. I had plans to have dinner with my wife and sons at seven, which he had managed to derail. I thought

I could just go for one drink. I went with him because he was my best attorney. I sent him all the places that I couldn't go since I'd married.

I called my driver to tell him that I was ready. "Here, I can help," Robert said holding my arm, realizing that I was drunk.

I glared at him. He was my age, and good-looking. Dark straight hair and startling blue eyes. I'd never seen him with a woman, and he never talked about one particular one. A man's sexual preferences were none of my concern if he did the job.

I did a background check on him and everything turned out perfect. He came from a small town in Pennsylvania, moved to a small town in Texas, got his BA there, went on to graduate from Harvard Law at the top of his class. He made a fortune during the housing and banking crisis.

Finances in order. Clothes expensive, a bit over the top sometimes, but not exceptionally so. He had a mother and father and a younger sister. Nothing about him would raise a red flag, so I gave him an apartment in my building as part of his package.

He had been working for me for two years, and in that time I'd never invited him out or to my home for dinner.

His conversations were all about women every time I saw him. He even asked when he could meet Alex. That was when I knew that he wasn't gay. Anyone who saw Alex would remark how lucky I was. I caught him staring at her picture one day and then he would smile, and say that he wished he could find someone as understanding and beautiful as Alex. Whereas I remarked that there was none like her.

"Let's go, Blackstone." The limo sat parked out front. We climbed in and had a brief conversation about my children, Maxim and Jack.

"There's this private club that's terrific. We should go there." I looked at him too drunk to reject his idea. "You won't be disappointed." I raised an eyebrow. I never enjoyed socializing with anyone who worked for me, unless it was something I wanted from them, or they were of a particular use to me.

"Don't worry, it's discreet," he said, grinning at me.

"All you have to do is relax and enjoy yourself. I've arranged everything."

"It's not that, Robert. You know I'm a married man."

"But you're not dead," he said.

"I will be if my wife finds out about this."

"Trust me she won't find out anything." Robert handed my driver an address. It was located off Park Avenue. "We can park in the private garage."

My limo took a hard left and Robert opened the garage door. The car came to a stop in garage space 1905. We exited the car, my head began to swirl, and I stumbled. "Whoa," I said. I think I had too much to drink. I'd better get home."

"No. You're not leaving me. Everyone's expecting you." He put my arm around his neck and helped me into the elevator. I glanced at him. He had drunk as much as I did, but he was on his feet and I could barely walk.

"Who is everyone?" I asked puzzled.

"A few friends. They mentioned that they had seen a picture of you in the papers, so I couldn't help but brag about you being my boss. They want to meet a billionaire." Somehow Robert convinced me that it was an innocent party. We entered the building on the nineteenth floor. He opened the door of apartment 1905 and then we stepped in. It was dark but for a few sconces hanging on the wall. The curtains were closed and the furniture sparse. A woman opened one of the rooms and walked out wearing a leather garment. It was a leather bra and bikini with six-inch black boots with a sheer robe covering her figure. I stood in surprise and asked Robert, "What is this?"

"I promised you a great time. You said that you were into BDSM on your last drink and your wife... Well... Why don't you settle down and enjoy yourself?" He pushed me on the sofa, and I fell like a rock.

The woman leaned in handing me a drink. I didn't take it, shaking my head no.

"I shouldn't have told you my personal business. Where are you going?"

"Just stay here until I return," Robert said smiling at me, then leaving the room.

"It's okay," she said, caressing my hair. "You can relax and enjoy yourself without anyone knowing. I know what you like. You don't have to worry about me. I'm discreet," the young woman said to me pressing her breasts in my face. I had never been so aroused since I first met Alex. But the tension of being a father and husband was taking its toll on me, and I convinced myself that I needed to relax.

I thought, *Why not?* The woman handed me the drink again and I took it, piling more Scotch and sodas on top of an already-saturated mind and body. When I woke, I was in a room with Robert looking down at me. The room was dark and swirling around. I couldn't tell if it was day or night, and frankly I didn't know, and I was beginning not to care.

I sat up and realized that I was naked, and the beautiful woman was lying down next to me. When she opened her eyes, sat up, and began trailing her long nails down my chest, she squeezed my nipple. I didn't respond, because my reaction to pain was not the same as others. Robert disappeared before I could protest.

I didn't question why I was lying naked, but I knew that my sexual addiction had returned full force. It was time to get to my psychologist for a session, but first, I was here, and like all addicts who promised to change, I needed one last intoxicating mind-blowing round.

I lay back and forgot about Alex, I forgot the dinnertime we shared as a couple. I wasn't happy about our arrangement. I piled on excuse after excuse. She said that we had to discuss our marriage after two years, and if it wasn't working for either one, then we were going to get a divorce. I was thinking now that I had been a disappointment to her. I was beginning to question what I was doing married anyway.

I placed my hands on the woman's soft skin and she turned and looked at me. "What's the matter? Am I not doing what you want?"

"I need more. You understand what I truly need, don't you?"

She reached on the nearest nightstand and gathered a pair of handcuffs. I lay on my back and she cuffed me to the bed, then she reached for a whip, and began lashing my back. "Harder. Harder," I confessed. I wanted to feel the pain. I knew I had engaged in something I promised Alex that would never occur, and now guilt haunted me.

The only way to take the guilt away was to beat it away. It was then that I knew I had to get home and make love to Alex. I hadn't had that feeling in a year. I needed the intensity of her body, I needed to be inside her.

The woman in the black garments took the handcuffs off, and asked, "Don't you want to fuck me?"

"I don't fuck anyone but my wife."

After my session, I paid her for her night's work and called Robert in.

"No one is to know about this," I said. He nodded and called for my car.

Chapter 12

Alex

It was almost 2 a.m. when Max came into our bedroom after he promised he would be home early. I turned over and watched him get undressed. Every time I looked over his body, I found myself almost climax. How could any man look that insanely gorgeous? He unbuttoned his white shirt, took time to stretch, and dropped his pants at the foot of our bed. I heard him open the door to the shower and stay there for an hour. I guessed he thought I was sleeping, and he could get in bed and leave one of his notes in the morning, and all would be forgotten when he reappeared.

I couldn't decide what to do, but when he slid in behind me, I felt his warm strong chest, his hard manhood on my butt, and his long arms reach and hold me close. A covering of relief lay over me, and I backed my behind into him and drifted off to sleep.

I woke early about 6 a.m. to check on the baby, and before I could turn and kiss him, I looked around and he had his back to me. My heart jumped from my chest. His back was covered with scars. I knew what that meant. He had been engaging in his usual masochistic activities.

"Did you fuck her?" I sat up, shouting. He woke startled out of a deep sleep, the kind he used to get from me.

"What? What is it, Alex?" He sat up in bed with that dark curly hair, which always looked like he had just been fucked by a harem of women. His impossibly green eyes never failed to arouse all kinds of feelings I never wanted to visit. I couldn't contain my jealousy and rage. Marrying Max hadn't mitigated the suspicion and doubt I was experiencing now.

"Do you know what your back looks like?" He sat up turned to me, and I slapped him. He didn't blink, he didn't react, but his face went blank, and his eyes closed for a second.

"I can explain," he said, gazing at me with those dark green eyes."

"What the fuck is this?" I said, examining his back. He tried to grab me and hold me.

"It's..."

"You don't have the decency to lie to me?"

"I can explain."

"What can you say that will make me believe you? Remember, I was the woman who knew your darkest secrets, and the beatings were one of them. I thought this was over."

"Can you understand, I was under pressure?"

"This is what you do every time you get pressure. You find a woman to beat you?"

"I didn't fuck her. She..."

"I would have preferred that you did. Then I would know that you didn't want me, and this would have been easy on all of us."

"What do you mean?"

"I warned you, Max. It's in the contract. You are a stickler for contracts and I'm holding you to it." I pushed out of the bed and stood over him.

"You can't do this," Max said hopping out of bed, rushing to grab my hands. I pulled my hands from his grasp.

"You can't separate from me. What about my boys?"

"You should have thought about them before you disappeared for two days. I want you out of my house."

"You can't do that, Alex."

"I'm not a little girl anymore. If you don't leave, I'm taking my sons and leaving here."

"You can take anything you want," Max said begging. "I'm nothing without you." He stood in the same spot looking down like a lost boy. "What am I going to do without you and my boys?"

"You don't see us anyway," I said reaching for my robe, feeling naked with my own husband. I tightened the belt on the pink-and-black silk robe and looked into his eyes. "I have money of my own from my mother's estate, so that will not be necessary. Give your money to your sons. I want to be rid of you. I can't live like this with you."

He reached for me as I passed him, and he brought me into his arms. "I want to make love to you," he said, his eyes brimming with heat with a dangerous blank stare. He stood focusing and staring down at my breasts. He held my hands behind my back, and I couldn't move. His mouth on my nipples, and my enlarged nipples responded to the warmth and tightening of his lips.

"You do want me," he said.

"I haven't had a man make love to me in months. You have been fucking me, not making love to me, and I don't think you know the difference anymore." He released my hands. I didn't want him to release me. I wanted him to make me believe him. I wanted him to tell me something. Lie to me. I was open for a lie after my betrayal.

"I knew St. John would pull us apart," Max said in total frustration.

"He had nothing to do with this, it was all you, Max." Wasn't that a lie? How did you reconcile with yourself that you were doing this to make way for another man. And all you thought about was that man. Did I find an excuse to punish Max for my indiscretions?

MAX

What was I thinking? What was wrong with me? The minute everything was going well, I did something uncharacteristic and stupid. I decided to leave the apartment and take residence at our private apartment, because I didn't want to cause Alex any more pain than necessary. I must make an appointment with the doctor.

I would get to see my sons and Alex today, I couldn't wait.

Doctors Office

"Max, sit. I haven't seen you in six months. Have you been taking your medication as I've prescribed?"

"Yes. Yes. I don't think it's working," I said, looking down at my hands. I noticed they were shaking. "That's not why I'm here," I said, praying he couldn't read the expressions on my face.

"Yes, I know. I heard from your wife. She made an appointment to see me."

Did Alex let me think that I was the one who had broken our marriage and sexual contract? Was she having an affair? *No.* I answered my own question.

"Mr. Blackstone, you appear to be deep in thought. Do you want to continue this session another day?" I agreed, stood, nodded, and hurried to the door.

"Take your medication," I heard as I bolted out of his office, rushing for the elevator. I opened the door and there stood Robert.

"What are you doing here, Robert, and in this building?" I thought nothing of it, but it was curious. Was he having me followed?

"I'm seeing my doctor," he said to me. "I'm surprised to see you here, Blackstone. I guess we all have some skeletons in our closets," he said with a forced smile. I shook his hand and thought nothing of it. After all, now he knew as much about me as I knew about him, but I had more to lose, and he had a lot to gain.

Alex

I didn't know what to tell the children. I sent their father away because he had a problem. Children didn't care about their parents' problems. Boys just wanted their father.

Max was gone most of the time. I didn't see him anyway. I tried to rationalize my behavior.

I would have a discussion with him. Maybe I could continue to live with him, for the sake of the children. He would have his room and I would have mine. This was the only way I could salvage my broken marriage. *Do I want to?* is the question.

What about the attractive man I thought about night and day? What was I to do with him? I needed to go on with my life, meet different people, maybe get a job. However, I'd been toying with the idea of going back to college, there was this law degree I'd started. Maybe I'd take a few classes until the boys were old enough.

I dressed and headed for the dreaded elevator. Since when had I been afraid to take my elevator in my own building? The day Robert came into my life was my answer. But he was not in my life and he was nothing to me. I tried convincing myself of the not so obvious.

I felt miserable when I didn't see Robert. I felt betrayed. Did I want to see him, or didn't I? Did I crave his attention? Did I crave being close to him, and why did I feel this way? *"Come on get yourself together,"* I mumbled. I took a cab instead of calling Brandon. Today I was going to Columbia University, and registering for one class. That should be easy.

⎯⎯⎯◦⎯⎯⎯

I STOPPED BY THE COUNSELOR'S office to make sure I'd chosen the right professors and check on the number of credits I might need if, or when I graduated. I wasn't fooling myself, this was just so I didn't have to think about Robert, the man I had become inadvertently infatuated with.

On leaving Ms. Williams's office, I had my papers in my hand and I wasn't paying attention to my surroundings, and I bumped into a young woman about my age, maybe a little younger. I recognized the look on her face, all excited about starting college, because she was me once.

"I'm sorry, my fault," she said with a wide warm grin.

"No. It's my fault," I said helping her retrieve her purse, and gathering the spilled contents scattered across the tile floor. I kneeled reaching and dropping in her purse a compact with eyeshadow, lipstick, perfume, numerous makeup items, including an assortment of candy. Glancing at her shoulder bag, she had money, or the purse was a knockoff, but I doubted that. When placing a pair of glasses in it, I did a closer inspection, and it was indeed real.

She had a genuine look about her, a soft welcoming innocent smile as if she needed a friend. I gave her a once over. Her jeans and shirt, expensive. Her shoes more expensive, therefore, the purse was more likely the real thing.

She needed a friend, and I could use someone my age to talk to.

"Thanks," she said. "How about having some coffee with me?" I looked at her. "My treat," she said with her sincere blue eyes beaming, regarding me and my clothing.

She probably thought I couldn't afford a cup of coffee. I was dressed in old cheap jeans and a sweatshirt. The ones I boxed up because I couldn't bear to leave them. I wanted to remember where I had come from and where I was going, and I didn't want to call any unnecessary attention to myself. I even found one of my faux black bags before Max convinced me that I needed to dress according to my status, which was the wife of the second-richest man in New York.

"Sure. Give me a few minutes to freshen up," I said to her.

"I'm coming with you, need to use the restroom," she said with a wide smile. Her teeth told a story, she was well taken care of, and her haircut was expensive.

"What about the counselor?" I asked her.

"I don't need to see her, all I have to do is select my classes and email my selection to her. My family donates gobs of money to this school. Oh. My name is Melody Silverstone,

"Alex short for Alexander... Blackstone," I said, holding out my hand. Instead she hugged me as if we were old friends meeting after a long absence.

"No kin to that Blackstone who owns most of Manhattan."

"Of course not. Do I look like I could be related to him?" She shot me a closed smile and grabbed my arm and tucked it under hers, "I hear he's a freak. I wish I could meet him one day."

"And where did you hear that?" I asked as we walked into the restroom. I stood at the mirror, and she entered one of the stalls.

"My father said this when I was eavesdropping of course. He said that Blackstone has this place in Manhattan, which operates under his sponsorship, and all kinds of kinky stuff goes on there. It's maybe just gossip among old men," she said washing her hands, drying them, and looking in the mirror for a second.

Melody glanced at me, and her mouth didn't stop moving until we reached the small specialty deli. I was sure her father confused Jonas with Max. This happened all the time. Max's name has been sullied by Jonas from the west coast, and now on the east coast. I would have to talk to Jonas.

"Here we are. What do you want? Remember I'm footing the bill."

"Only coffee." After we sat, Melody chattered and gossiped about people I'd never heard of, or wasn't interested in. I knew never to tell her any secrets. We had been sitting there for an hour. I reached for my purse.

"Oh, you're not leaving?" she said, her voice showing disappointment.

"I have to get back to my children."

"You have children?" Her face lit up.

"Yes. Two boys. My husband and I are separated."

"Oh. Too bad. A broken home. My mother wanted to leave my father, but she stayed because of me." And Melody talked for another hour about how her father was a womanizer, and her mother wished that he was just a plain old freak. "You know..." she continued, "...one of those men who love to be beaten, and then she could take out her anger on him." She paused to take a breath.

"Sorry, Melody, but I must leave now. My sons, remember," I said apologizing to her.

"I understand. I hope we get classes together," she said. I glanced at her and smiled. It was the first time in a year I'd had conversations with a woman my age, and for some reason I enjoyed her aimless nonstop chit chat.

Classes were to begin in a week, and I was excited about it all. I would have something to keep my mind off Max and Robert, and still have time to be with my boys and my little dog.

Chapter 13

I hadn't seen Robert in weeks. Maybe he didn't lie when he said he was on vacation. I found myself missing him more than Max. But how could that happen? Robert had women coming and going, and still I didn't judge him as harshly as I was judging Max. Was it because Max was my husband, or I had some underlying reason in my subconscious I wasn't ready to address? Was it possible I was reacting because I was jealous of the women being a part of Robert's life and I was not? Robert had managed to ignite feelings of envy, anger, and jealousy in me.

Feelings I thought were dormant and ridiculous.

I was up early having my morning breakfast, because I had one class at 10 a.m. today, and one on Wednesday at 6 p.m. I hurried out because the doorman had called a taxi, and the driver was waiting for me at the curb.

I had to remember to contact Jonas today, and ask him about the rumors surrounding Max concerning his club, not that I expected the truth, but somewhere in Jonas's explanations I could peel away his lies and find some truth.

Excited on my first day of class, I checked to see if I had everything I needed in my backpack. I dressed in worn jeans and white shirt and a pair of cheap sneakers. Somehow I was happy I didn't see that man who had me nervous whenever I was near him. Checking the time, I was early for class.

I found the large lecture hall and took a seat in the back. As the hall began to fill, I looked at the schedule. Looking at the seats and the large number of students filing in, he must be good. Then out of nowhere my eyes locked on Melody's. She waved and headed up the stairs where I was sitting.

"Can you believe this?" she said, breathing hard from running up the stairs.

"No. Not on your life would I believe that I would ever see you again." I knew then if we continued to sit together that nothing would get done, and I could drop this class today, because I would fail the course, because although I enjoyed her company, she was distracting with her continuous conversations.

After dropping her backpack in a seat to her right, I placed mine to the left of me, then she sat next to me. "I hear the professor is a real hunk." I glanced at the schedule.

"It's Dr. Healy's class. He's seventy," I said, looking at her a bit surprised. She couldn't find a seventy-year-old man hot? Or could she? These days, nothing would surprise me on what turned some people on.

"I know. He had a heart attack, and they called in this lawyer at the last minute for a favor. He's taking over Dr. Healy's class. By the discussion going around school, this guy is a handsome freak. He has fucked most of the women in this class, that is, everyone except me, and you, I guess." I raised my chin, bit my lip, shooting her a look of disbelief. "Seriously, Alex. He's so rich and good-looking that women are dropping their panties for him in droves. But in some cases the women aren't wearing anything but a thong, if that."

"How do you know all of this?"

"I eavesdrop on my mother when she's talking to her friends. Some of the women are on Columbia's board, and they are heavy donors, and men too shoot the breeze with my mother, that is they gossip. They tell her everything that's going on around here. I guess old women just like to gossip about young men, because they aren't getting any."

"It's not just old women. Some young women are having the same problem." I shot her a look and raised an eyebrow, but her expression never changed. "And listening to all the womanizing this professor is doing, I don't want to be caught dead in his bed," I said to Melody.

"Me. I'd like to find out what turns him on. Anytime you see a man with that many women, someone isn't doing the job right or giving him what he likes. I wonder if he likes a little BDSM. I'd like to whip his ass sometime."

"Oh, Melody," I said, closing my eyes for a second.

"Straight up. I would do it in a fast second. And suck his dick and let him fuck me here there and everywhere."

"Get out of here," I said smiling, pushing her shoulder, "Oh my god, I can't believe what I'm hearing." I began to laugh because I couldn't believe anyone was that free to express herself so openly. I gazed at the students sitting in the next two seats, wondering if they had heard her. A female student sat texting and appeared to be in her own world and the guy next to her, he had a conversation going on with his mother.

I'd had an open mind since I'd met and married Max. I had forgotten how twenty-something women talked among themselves.

"I'm dead serious, Alex. I would use a dildo on him in a minute if he was into that."

"No?"

"Yes. In a second. Then I would let him eat me out and see what kind of skills he had, and if they were lacking, then I would teach him how to satisfy me. You can't have a man going down on you and doing all kinds of nasty stuff if he has no skills. You can get hurt.

Why a girlfriend had her clit bit off just because her boyfriend didn't have a clue, and he didn't know that it was attached to her. Come to find out she was his first and last. Word got around and neither one could get a date. So they had to stay together," Melody said, hunching her shoulders.

"No. I don't believe you."

"Well, it makes a good story anyway. And why ruin a good story with the truth?" She glanced at me with a grin and took a drink of her diet coke from a straw, the sound making a loud annoying noise. Then she opened the top of the cup and reached in and took out a small ice cube. Turning to me, holding it and waving it around, before plopping it into her mouth, she said, "You know these are good for making love."

"No, I didn't know."

"What you could do with these," she said, cracking one cube with her teeth. "My boyfriend put these on my—"

"I get the picture," I said, conveniently interrupting her.

"Okay. Don't call me up and ask me how to use them, because you had your chance."

I thought I might have hurt her feelings. Melody became quiet, opened a book, and pretended she was reading it. She must have taken me for a prude and thought I needed a lesson on how to get an orgasm.

All I needed to do was ask her a question and she started again. Melody's banter on the joys and power of lovemaking made the half hour pass quickly. I glanced down at my phone for the time and in walked, and from where we sat in the cheap seats, I had to put my glasses on to see him. I could see he was tall with a full head of brilliant dark hair, the kind you wanted to run your hands through as he was ravishing your breasts or going down on you. The "just-fucked, I don't care, I want you to know I fucked" hair, appeared awfully familiar.

He stood behind his computer gazing at the crowd. When he spoke, I knew that voice. "I'm passing around the roster, please sign it. If you don't, I will assume that you didn't show up for class, and as you can see it is very large and I will be very busy.

"He'll be busy alright, fondling someone's ass," Melody whispered, leaning close to my ear.

"If any of you are planning on dropping out, I suggest you do it now." No one stood. They turned looking at the next guy and remained in their seats. Then his eyes focused on me and for the life of me, I couldn't tell how he knew I was there, but he said, "Mrs. Blackstone, I need to see you after class." And then I remembered he would have a list of all the students in the class.

"Dr. Healy's syllabus is on my class website. I suggest you download it and follow it to the letter."

Melody grabbed my leg, and whispered, "Oh, he has you in his sights. He's good. I bet he knows everyone he has fucked in here and you aren't one of them."

I still wasn't sure it was him because of the way he was dressed. He wore a plain white shirt and jeans. But then... "My name is Professor Montgomery. You will get my syllabus tomorrow in your email box."

"Two syllabi?" Melody questioned. "I don't know. This is going to be harder than I thought."

I leaned over and whispered to Melody, "He lives in my building. I see him every day."

"Well, it shouldn't be a problem. You don't have to go far to fuck him. You are going to fuck him, aren't you?"

"I wouldn't fuck him if he wore two rubbers."

"That's what they all say. Look at that body, that hair, and lips."

"You can see his lips from here?"

"You can't have a face and body like that without having lips you want to bite and suck all day. I just imagine he is something in bed. Make sure you tell me about it when you do it with him. You are going to fuck him?" She glanced my way for an answer, or something that would reveal my intentions. "Think about our grades. I have to pass this class or else my parents will take away my allowance. Take one for the team." My eyes swung in her direction. Melody hunched her shoulders, "Talking too much to my father, so sue me," she said grinning.

Since when did this become our *grades*? I thought. The word *our* reminded me to call Jonas.

Robert lectured the entire two hours, which included a PowerPoint presentation. And then class was over, and it was time.

"I'm not going to see him," I whispered to Melody.

"But why?"

"You don't understand, Melody, and I don't have time to tell you," I said, standing and picking up my backpack, and draping it over one shoulder. "I have to get home to my boys."

"Good idea. He's going to his office and expecting you there. This will make him want you more," Melody said, as if she was hatching a plan. "We'll just slip out and you can go home. Do you need a ride?"

"No thanks, I can find my way. I'll just take a cab."

Chapter 14

I made it home about one thirty, my lunch was sitting out waiting for me, a chicken salad sandwich. I wasn't hungry. I needed to talk to Max. I checked his room, not expecting him to be there, and he wasn't. I agreed to live with him, hoping things would return to normal, but it didn't. He was just there to be around the boys and stop me from having another life. He was the only one benefitting from this arrangement. I must have been out of my mind to think this would work.

I really needed to talk to Max, because my life was spiraling out of control. The life I wanted with him, my desire for him was fading the more I thought of Robert. I remembered when all I wanted was to be with Max, and for us to live as a family, but even that wasn't working. "I better try Jonas. Maybe he has heard from him," I murmured to myself.

"May I speak with Jonas Blackstone?"

"He's not here," a man's coarse voice answered, throwing me for a loop. Most times Jonas would answer, because he expected a call from Crystal, and she should be having her baby about now.

"Well, when will he be available?"

"I don't know, maybe never." And he hung up. What was going on with Jonas now? I hoped he didn't get himself in trouble again, but wait, this was Jonas, and he was always in trouble. That was his middle name Jonas Trouble Blackstone. This didn't sound too good. I decided to call Max at his office instead of texting him.

"Max. I've been calling you and calling."

"I know, but I am in negotiations now." Max didn't sound like himself. As a matter of fact he sounded more like Jonas."

"Jonas? Is that you?"

"Alex, how did you know?"

"Never mind that," I said. "Have you seen Max?"

"Something terrible has happened."

"What?" I shook my head and slumped into the chair near my bed. *What now?*

"I'm coming over there."

"Why?" And the phone went blank. I would have to sit around and wait on Jonas to find out what had happened to Max. I couldn't sit still. I walked and walked, cried, and paced the room, waiting to hear from Jonas.

———◆———

AN HOUR PASSED AND finally the doorman buzzed, and I ran to get the message. He announced that I had a visitor. "Let him in," I said, not asking who he was. I waited until I heard the door to the elevator, then I opened the door, and standing in front of me was Jonas. He had a look on his face of a sad little boy. Jonas always wore that expression, especially when he had done something to cause Max a problem, and that happened all the time in San Francisco.

This look was different. I had never seen such a look of despair on his face. He rushed past me, and reached for a bottle of Scotch from the liquor cabinet, and downed half a glass with no ice.

I glanced at him. "Haven't you kept me waiting long enough to hear about Max?" I just knew he would tell me that Max had left me for another woman, or something close to that. I held my breath, hoping it wasn't that, but it was much worse. I could tell by the look on Jonas's face.

"I think Max has been kidnapped. I went to his office to discuss my business and ask him for help. I stayed there in his office until today when you called."

My breathing ceased and I sucked in air. I wandered aimlessly to the liquor cabinet, and poured myself a drink. I sat with the glass in my hand. "Why do you think this?" I asked. "Max has two bodyguards and a chauffeur. There is no way this can happen. And no one knows about me and the children except you. I hope you haven't put my children in jeopardy," I said, staring up at Jonas, his face usually an open book, but for some reason I couldn't figure him out. His face was blank. Was this his soldier's expression during interrogation, a planned effort to conceal information from the enemy?

He managed to survive his combat mission after his company had been destroyed. What was behind the mask of good-natured Jonas, he so easily revealed some days, and on other days, was a paradox?

"I think Max can take care of himself. There is no way anyone can get to him." I glanced at Jonas with a raised eyebrow, "But if they thought he was me, then..." Jonas said, trying to concede something before I interrupted him.

"Why would someone think he was you? Is there something you're keeping from me?" I questioned, my eyes narrowing. Jonas had begun to fidget with his hands, then he stood and paced around the room, taking time to look aimlessly through the panoramic window.

"Do you have a cigarette?" he said with his back to me still facing the window. Now I knew something was up with him. He stopped smoking cigarettes when he kicked his drug and alcohol habit. Now he was drinking and smoking. This could be serious. I rushed over to him and took the empty glass from his hand.

"Tell me, Jonas. What did you do?" I shouted. My heart was about bursting through my chest. I had to hold my body to keep from trembling. I realized then that without Max I didn't want to go on. What would life be without him? Without Max I had nothing. Tears pooled in my eyes and all the breath flowed out and I felt lightheaded. I held on to the chair, breathing hard.

Jonas walked around the room in a circle and came back to stand in front of me.

"Stop shaking your hands," I shouted, my voice weak between tears. "Now tell me, and don't leave anything out."

He sat near me. I didn't want him anywhere close to me, especially at times like these. He tried to stop his feet from shaking and his hands, but he was losing the battle. "I asked Max to come to my office, because I wanted to discuss a financial matter with him. I had to step out and he was waiting for me, but by the time I returned, he was gone. I think he was mistaken for me and kidnapped.

"Why would anyone want to do this?" He glanced at me. "I think it's because of you?"

Silence blanketed the room. We sat staring at each other. I didn't want to ask, I was afraid to ask. I wanted to run and hide in my bedroom and not come out. I didn't want this life anymore, I wanted another life. A life that was quiet. I should have stayed in Montana with Max. I had to come to New York. Now I didn't have Max.

I went through a slew of regrets until I heard a key in the door. I grabbed Jonas's hand and held it tight. We were both afraid.

There standing in front of me dressed all in black was Maximillian Blackstone smiling. "Well, what's going on Mrs. Blackstone, did you miss me so much that you had to take up with this cardboard copy of me?" he asked smiling, and Jonas rushed to his brother and held him tight as if he didn't want to let him go.

"I love you, too, Jonas," Max said, pulling away from Jonas's grip and making his way to me. "What's the matter, baby, you act as if you have seen a ghost?" Jonas and I glanced at each other.

"Max. I'm ready to leave New York when you are. This minute if possible."

"Hold your horses, baby. There are a few more things I will put in order, and we can go home." Max glanced down at me holding on to him for dear life. By the look on his face he didn't know what to make of my sudden change. But he knew when he had won, and he wasn't going to push it by asking questions.

ALEX

Jonas and I tucked away another one of our conspiracies and secrets. We didn't talk about it with Max. What good would it do? Although Jonas was wrong about the kidnapping, there was something simmering below, and it had to do with me. For now, I just didn't want to know about it or think about it. Max promised me that we could leave New York soon. I thought that would be my salvation. Get away, go back to Montana where all this started and make a fresh start.

I'd been depressed every day and needing him. Max had been away from us for weeks. He was flying in today, and he was taking the boys out and he said he was bringing a friend. I'd seen him more now than in the last year and he spent more time with the children. We were having vanilla sex as Max described it, and it was extremely hot for me.

Max took the time to bring me flowers and candy, aside from all the expensive gifts he forced on me. I hoped this was enough for him. But deep down I hoped it was enough for me.

I didn't think about Robert as I used to. He was standing in the way of my love for Max. Once Max said we would be leaving to go back to Montana, I cancelled my classes. I would miss Melody as she was the brightest thing about being in New York. I'd have to get in touch with her and explain. Knowing Melody, it shouldn't be that hard to contact her, considering everyone's life was plastered all over social media sites. And she was probably the type to have all her pictures and information on Instagram and Twitter.

Max would be here at 11 a.m. He was taking the children to the Christmas show at Radio City Music Hall and they were all excited. Two weeks ago he took them to the zoo, and they couldn't stop their little chatter about the animals.

The children were dressed and waiting with Lapita. I swiped lip gloss on my lips and threw on a dress with a V-cut neckline and my Christian Louboutin shoes, the ones with the red heels. I liked to tease him when he came home after being away. That was his punishment, that and vanilla sex, and a marriage counselor.

I wondered what he would do to me if he ever found out about my indiscretions. I wasn't going to think about that anymore. I was going to put an end to this today, and hopefully bury that body so deep, no one could dig it up. I heard the buzzer and Lapita rushed for the door. I heard the children's little voices. They were screaming, "Daddy. Daddy." I rushed out and stopped in my tracks. My expression changed.

"Alex, this is my good friend, Robert." I turned chalky, my hands were sweaty.

"It's nice to make your acquaintance, Mrs. Blackstone." I looked at him, my eyes glazing over. I was in a daze. My worst nightmare. It was him standing in my house with a white pullover under a midnight-blue leather jacket and dark-blue wool slacks hugging his sculpted hips. I couldn't tell which one was more handsome than the other, Max or Robert. Seeing them together was mesmerizing. Downright scary. And I was hot for both and they were hot for me. I could see it in their eyes, and they were both blind because they thought that my smile was for only one of them.

Max was standing dressed in a black silk shirt opened at the collar, and a black coat and silk and wool black pants. "Robert came along to help me with my boys." I was thinking, *He came along to help you with more than just our boys.*

"It's a pleasure to meet you, Robert. Where did you meet my husband? I never heard him talk about you." I didn't extend my hand. My cheeks were red and my hands sweaty. I couldn't handle the tell-tale sign of arousal, the sign of want and need.

The children were pulling Max's hand and ready to go. "We have to leave now." Robert took them out. "I need to speak to my wife," Max's words and smile innocent yet taunting for Robert. He reacted and I knew immediately his feelings.

Robert gave a quick nod, never answering my question, and appeared to be relieved that he didn't have to answer it. He hurried into the foyer with the children, holding my baby, Jack, in his arms.

"Alex, you look so... so lovely," Max whispered with his nose trailing down my neck heading for my breasts. Max stood gazing at me as if he could pull me to the floor and take me there. Then he realized that we were not alone. "There is a function I need to attend, please say you will accompany me, it's on Saturday?" My eyes shut tight. "It's for a special cause. You said that I didn't take you anywhere." And he smiled his half-crooked smile with dimples digging into the sides of his face.

"That was before..." He stopped me.

"How many times can I say I'm sorry?"

"I'll agree if you go with me to a marriage counselor?" I said to him. He held my hand, and I walked him to the door. Robert turned, stark steel-blue eyes covering me. I pulled back away from Max. It was as if I was betraying Robert with Max. *We aren't having an affair, so why am I feeling as if something is going on between us?* I asked myself. *I must stop this. I have to get my marriage back on track.*

Max grabbed my hand and held it to his mouth, and said with his brooding eyes looking down at me, "Anything. Anything you want I'll do it. I can't imagine losing you. I don't know what I would do." Then his face changed, and he gave me a faint smile.

He held the door and was ready to leave when he turned, and said, "Don't forget, Alex, it's a black-tie affair, wear your most expensive gown and jewels. Oh, I forgot," he said, putting his fingers to his forehead. Robert will accompany us. Robert spends his days and nights working for my company and hasn't had time to meet anyone. I gave him an apartment in this building as part of his package, a signing bonus."

That's old news. Did Robert think I was I part of the package? I couldn't help adding that to my thoughts as I gazed quietly at Robert playing with my children.

"He's going to take over my companies and run them from New York, so I can devote more time to you. We can go back to Montana, and I don't have to take time away from you and the boys."

I hadn't seen Max that happy in years, however, I hadn't been this miserable in years. Now that I was trying to rid myself of Robert, he managed to cajole and scheme to get into our lives. Max kissed me lightly on my lips, and whispered in my ear, "When I come back, I'm going to tie you up and crawl between those beautiful, alluring legs, and never come up for air."

Maybe Max took too long saying goodbye to me, because Robert turned, saw me blush red, and he regarded me with his blue eyes, and when Robert handed Max our baby, Max turned his back, and Robert facing me, shot me an icy wicked smile and a scandalous wink.

It wasn't too extreme in thinking that Robert had a jealous nature, and he was indeed jealous of my relationship and marriage to Max. I recognized that in him, but I wasn't a jealous person, and I didn't know the nature of a jealous man, but I heard it could be deadly.

The End

"Passion is a great love story."

Book 5: Mourning Becomes Black

Thank you for reading my book. You can connect with me on my blog or website at:

http://www.rachel-e-rice.com or contact me at rachelerice04@gmail.com. Book 1 in the Blackstone series is free everywhere you buy your books. Please leave a review. Below you will find a list of my books and they can be bought at all eBook stores. Following the list of books is an excerpt from book 1 of The **Blackstone Series: The Incredible Mr. Black**

Blackstone Books by Rachel E Rice

Erotic Romance

1. The Incredible Mr. Black
2. Temptation In Black
3. Submission To Black
4. Black Tie Affair
5. Mourning Becomes Black
6. Fade To Black
7. Back To Black
8. Black Tide
9. Black Swan
10. Black Out

Prologue

The Incredible Mr. Black Book 1
By Rachel E Rice

The worst thing a young woman could do was fall in love, and worse yet was to fall in love with a sexy, drop-dead gorgeous rich man. Because you could find yourself doing things you never would imagine—like letting him handcuff you to his bed as he made passionate, erotic love to you.

Driving into the gated community, shivering from the thought, I stopped to put in the code. The mansion was set on a lush, green, manicured hill with a circular driveway. I stopped and exited my SL 550 Mercedes, another present I accepted from the billionaire industrialist, Maximilian Blackstone, or as I called him, Mr. Black.

The valet reached for my keys. I stiffened my hand. He felt my hand hesitate. "Don't worry, Miss. We'll take care of your car." It wasn't the car that worried me.

Walking in a daze, I was now at the front door of Pandora's Retreat, a luxurious getaway for the serious bondage and S& M enthusiast. My mind wavering as I counted my steps, I couldn't decide whether I wanted to do this—whether I wanted to walk through those double glass doors with the gold-plated trim and spend a week experiencing a world of BDSM.

I'd had only one man in my sexual life, and I couldn't imagine anyone who could match the incredible Mr. Black, or Max, as his friends called him.

I tugged the collar of my cream-colored silk shirt and lumbered on through the doors. My gaze turned, following an attractive woman heading in my direction. A faint light bounced off her stern face. She stopped to greet me. "Welcome, Ms. Johns. You will find your stay most delightful, and you will discover that we have attended to all your needs, including an apartment for a week's stay." The director, a beautiful, golden-haired woman of forty, wearing a black fitted dress and high heels, who appeared to enjoy her job, smiled warmly, opening the door of the apartment and handing me the key.

How has it come to this? Why did I agree to do this? I wondered, ignoring the answer.

Three years ago, I fell in love, and the last thing I thought about was being a sex slave to a beautiful, exotic-looking billionaire. He appeared normal on the outside, but by my standards then, there was nothing normal about whippings, ropes, and handcuffs. I guessed a few years ago, I would have been considered vanilla.

I was here to meet the Master. He was going to teach me how to be the perfect sub and bring me to a higher level of submission. Mr. Black suggested that I was confused, and I didn't know whether I was a sub or a Domme, and he needed a sub. I knew what I was; he just couldn't handle it. Finally I agreed to his wishes, but I warned him that sending me here could be dangerous for both of us. But deep down inside, I was anxious to learn about the real world of bondage. Until now, I had been faking it to understand and fit into the world of my incredible Mr. Black.

When did this begin? I asked myself as I prepared my mind and body for what I had come to love. When did I begin to enjoy a man placing me over his knee, whipping my ass, and tying me to his headboard while fucking me senseless?

It started the day I answered an ad in the local newspaper for a terrific job in Montana, never bothering to read the small print.

Chapter 1

On the first day of the job, I was suffering from jet lag, incompetence, identity crisis, and a host of other insecurities, as I was a twenty-two-year-old who had just completed college with mountains of debt, and no friends or family to speak of. I had found the position in the *New York Post*: *Wanted—young, gregarious go-getter to work in sales. She should be intelligent, a college graduate, pretty without being noticeable, comfortable with individuals who are among the one percent...*The ad went on and on. I figured I had one of the qualities they advertised, so I packed my bags and headed to Billings, Montana, in the middle of ski season.

I wasn't a drop-dead gorgeous woman, but I had my charms. I was just average, with long, curly auburn hair often worn in a ponytail, an oval face, high cheekbones, and large blue eyes. I never trusted my looks as a magnet for men.

I never got the impression that the company that hired me was more interested in my looks than whether I could do the job.

"Ms. Bishop," the manager, Joshua, said, holding my resumé and looking over his glasses, "...can you work overtime?" That was it. Staring at him as his eyes glanced intermittently at me, I thought he was a great-looking guy with dirty-blond hair and a taut body. The kind of body you would get from farm work, not spending time in a gym.

They must have been desperate for personnel, but you couldn't tell by the beautiful scenery, luxurious accommodations for the staff and guests, and endless supply of food. The pay was great, though I would have paid *them* to work at Blackstone Ski Lodge.

I soon learned that the altitude was unbearable, and on one occasion I almost fainted. My skin stayed dry, and I had to keep a supply of Vaseline and ChapStick in my imitation-leather purse. I was constantly licking my lips and batting my eyes because I wasn't used to makeup. One of the hotel guests, an older gentleman, thought I was flirting with him. He was about seventy. "Get a life," I said.

Shuffling off none too happy, he tried to have me fired, but Joshua intervened, and that was why he and I became best buds. Besides, he let me sleep on his couch because I was afraid to live alone. I was sure he expected much more, but that was all I had to give. I planned on remaining a virgin until the right man came along. I wanted a handsome and rich man but that was just a dream. The problem was, it was as easy to fall in love with a rich man as a poor one, but probabilities were that I would never meet a rich, handsome man who would even look at me and say, "She's the one."

It was the middle of the winter ski season, and the hotel was shorthanded. Joshua took his time getting to the counter because he liked his long lunches with the newly hired. He claimed he wanted to do a detailed interview. I knew better, but I owed him just for taking a chance on me.

Reaching for my ChapStick under the counter, I stooped, and when I raised my head, I gazed directly into the eyes of the most gorgeous man I had ever seen. Living in New York, I had seen my share of men. I had seen all races, all nationalities, all ages, gay and straight, and he was just beautiful. A face like none I have ever seen. He had wide, dark-green eyes, a strong jaw, a head full of dark curls cut short, and thick eyebrows, and he wore a hidden smile, or was that a smirk, the kind I had seen on a billboard for Tom Ford Noir?

Yes, Noir. It means black—how fitting.

He was different. I felt it throughout my body. My legs tingled, my hands shook, and my mouth opened wide. He was *the one.* The one I would do anything for, the one I would give up my virginity for in a fast second if he only asked with just a whisper in my ear.

This did not say much about my self-control. I thought I had plenty until I laid eyes on him. "Wow!" His breathtaking, sinful face should have been concealed to prevent him from casting a spell on all women who gazed into his green eyes. Those eyes appeared capable of seeing through a woman's dress and straight to her clit.

He had been chatting and laughing as he glided into the lodge, but he paused when our eyes locked. He stopped in his tracks, there was a moment of silence, and then his gaze wandered around the room, which filled again with idle chatter.

I knew he was trouble when I scanned his gorgeous face and body. He strutted through a throng of eligible obscenely beautiful young men and women with all eyes targeting him. They leaned and whispered. Obviously, they knew him. Dressed immaculately in a black Giorgio Armani suit, a black-and-white Prada shirt, and black Gucci loafers, he strolled with a sort of swagger, leaning as he walked silently and quickly like a predatory cat, through the double glass doors of the lodge, with an entourage of three handsome men trailing behind his muscular ass. His curly jet-black hair was tousled and windswept, his piercing green eyes begging me to lie down and stay awhile to be his sex slave on call, I thought. "Wow."

This man was a sinful delight for any woman crazy enough to fall in love with him. So I convinced myself to keep my wits about me and not act like a frigging idiot. *It's far too late for that,* I admitted.

Joshua returned just in time. "Sorry, Alex, I owe you one."

"Oh, that's okay," I said, following that handsome fuck's gaze. I heard nothing and saw nothing; I was staring into space, dreaming, walking from behind the counter, heading in the direction of the elevators, trying to get out of the room before I fainted.

The procession caught up with me and I nervously stepped aside to allow the entourage and that man I would die for in the elevator, hesitating, praying the door would close. Too soon, he turned around, his face expressive and light with a skillful grin, a disarming smile he used to great effect. Facing the open door and the space that I now occupied, he said, "What a delightful looking necklace on such an impeccable background." His voice, smooth sounding, enunciation perfect; his background, prep school, elite college, and university, seduced me, surprised me, and then the elevator closed immediately in my goofy-looking face.

My head gave a quick jerk downward to see what he was looking at. I grabbed for the turquoise drop held by a black string, the only piece of jewelry that I owned, and wondered, *What is it?* Why would a rich, handsome fuck like him admire a cheap piece of Indian jewelry?

As I passed the mirror, I noticed that a button had come undone, and a hint of my breasts were peeking through. I now became aware of what he had seen, taking the view in. "Not bad," I said, admiring my best assets. Thank God I wore my expensive Victoria's Secret bra with black lace trim. Thank God I had thrown out all my old, comfortable, ratty bras, otherwise, I would never be able to show my face again. I didn't feel so bad now, just embarrassed. I hoped he didn't think I did that on purpose. I bet woman were hiding around every corner throwing their panties in his direction. I knew I would if I had half the chance.

Scrambling to button my shirt and breathing deep with shame, I put my head down and scurried into the employees' lounge. I thought about him all night. Why did he have to notice me? Why did I have to look like a misfit around all those wonderful-looking rich people, and why did he have to make me feel so inadequate? *Couldn't he just keep that beautiful mouth with those perfect white teeth shut?*

Determine to ignore him the next day, I excused myself as soon as I saw him come out of the elevator with his entourage. I muttered something about needing to use the restroom and turned away when I saw him moving in the direction of the counter. He didn't send his secretary or one of his bodyguards. He sauntered up with all the confidence of a rich, handsome, arrogant thirty-something. I ducked low and scurried into the back office, hiding like a child who had just stolen her big sister's lipstick.

When I finally thought it was safe to come out, Freddie, the new hire, looked me up and down with a judgmental look in his brown eyes. "Mr. Blackstone asked for you."

"Did he tell you what he wanted?" It took a moment to register. "You mean…" and, "I was too…" I mumbled, looking up his room number. *Yes, the penthouse suite. Why didn't he take the private elevator?*

"People like that don't explain themselves," Freddie said, not looking up from the computer, "But he was awfully interested in you."

"What is his problem? Do you think he wants to fire me?" I asked, my voice shaky and shrill.

Freddie rolled his shoulders to his ears. "Well, he asked your name and whether you were married and did you have any friends? Quote, 'boyfriends.'" Freddie made quotation marks in the air. "Those were his exact words…" Freddie paused as I held my breath. "I told him that I didn't know."

"Why did you say that?" My eyes opened wide.

"Because I don't know and it's none of his business. Besides, I don't care how much money he has, he has no right to invade your privacy."

"Let me be the judge of that," I said under my breath, rolling my eyes.

The next day, standing at my desk and reading *The Great Gatsby*, a book I'd never read in college because CliffsNotes were easier, I felt eyes measuring me. It was an eerie feeling. When I glanced up, he was staring at me with those penetrating, deep, dark-green eyes. He had come from outside, and for once he was alone. He just stood looking at me, those jade eyes undressing me, leaving me weak.

My body shook, and blood coursed through my veins, forcing my blood pressure up. I felt faint; he appeared to have that effect on me whenever he was near. He opened his mouth, and the sight of those lips and perfect white teeth sucked out what oxygen was left in my brain. My eyes glanced up to his perfect nose, dark, layered eyebrows, and then back to his mouth, and I began daydreaming about where he could put those lips.

"Hello," he said, soft and smooth.

"Yes? Hello." I responded like the idiot I claimed I would never become if I laid eyes on him again.

"Ms. Bishop... I was wondering if... I want... I would like to see you," he said with a sexy English tone to his voice.

"Why?" I leaned forward. "Did you say you want to see me, sir—ah, Mr. Black... I mean, Mr. Blackstone?" I sounded incompetent, like I had escaped from an asylum.

"Forget it. I'm sorry," he said, fading away into the private elevator. I stood staring at the spot where he had asked to see me, my mouth so wide it could have caught a fly if any could have survived at this altitude. A man like that asking to see me—did he mean what I thought he meant? Me? Alexander Bishop, a girl who had never been anywhere except Brooklyn—well, I could count the states—breathing the same air as this rich, handsome, drop-dead gorgeous fuck. He looked all of thirty-five, so I rationalized that he was too old, too worldly, and too dangerous for me.

And what did he mean by "wanting to see me?" Was I reading too much in those few words? Joshua said I analyzed things to death. But I couldn't understand why a man who was obviously articulate would just say, "I want to see you."

If I was stupid enough to dream that he thought I was attractive or entertain such an idea, all I could do was get hurt. I had no defense. I wasn't worldly, I had one friend, I had no money, and I wasn't that pretty.

What kind of experience did I have even talking to that world-class man? Maybe he was married, and I would be one of the many girls he fucked on vacation, but for me it would be a fuck of a lifetime. I might never recover if he put his rich dick in me. I would be gone. *I'll probably turn into a stalker*, I thought. So, it was better that I get him out of my mind, but I couldn't. He haunted my thoughts and my body, especially my clit. A chill eased up my back, caressing my spine straight into the nape of my neck and settling in the roots of my hair. *Wow!* It was then I knew that I would do anything for him, and that was dangerous.

⸺⦿⸺

THE NEXT DAY I FIGURED the best way to rid myself of Mr. Black was to try out my new skis, maybe break a leg or something, and have them send me back to Brooklyn with workman's comp. That would help me until I could get another job and get far away from him.

I had lied on my application and stated that I was proficient on the slopes. So they gave me skis, and lessons were free to upgrade my skills. What skills? Bending forward, adjusting the skis, I stepped backward until I hit a wall, or so I thought. Looking through my legs, I saw a pair of skis with two long legs covered in a black ski suit behind me. It was Mr. Black's rock-hard body. There he stood, all six foot two in a black ski suit and gear, and my ass was plastered directly on his hard dick.

He didn't move. Through my legs, I saw his head tilt down. His gaze scanned my hair, my back, and my ass. By the look in his eyes, he appeared to be measuring the split of my butt for something, and I didn't know what. I couldn't straighten up; my finger had gotten stuck in my ski boots, and when I unhinged it and stood, he never moved. He stood on my skis with a wicked smile, and without moving an inch, I said wryly, "I hope you're enjoying yourself. Take a picture; it'll last longer." That was all I could think of.

"Well, Ms. Bishop..." he said with a sly smile crossing his inviting lips. "...we meet again," he said with his body close, so that not even a sheet of paper could pass between us, as if we were entwined in intercourse and he had penetrated my ass. He whispered softly in my ear, my butt quivering against his dick as he got even closer, if that was possible. He circled my body with his arms, and said, "You smell wonderful."

"Thank you, but could you get off of my skis?"

He moved his hand, caressing my chin, then placed it lower. "Your beautiful neck needs something: a collar," he stated casually, passing his fingers from the front to the back, causing me to shiver, not from the cold, but from the heat of his penis penetrating my clothing like lightning. At the time I thought nothing of his comments. Maybe that was what the rich said when they wanted to make a pass, and I responded in a childish and girlish manner.

"You smell pretty good yourself," was all I could get out and then I froze. I should have asked, *What the fuck are you doing?* But I didn't. I should have asked, *Have you lost your fucking mind?* But I didn't. I should have asked, *Do you think I'm that kind of girl? Do you want to fuck me?* But I didn't. I managed to slightly turn my head.

"I was wondering whether I can see you under different circumstances," he said with a hint of vulnerability dancing in his green eyes, which had softened.

"You are seeing me now. Why do you wish to see me? And please get off my skis," I said coldly, trying to cool the heat that was coursing between my thighs.

When I finally moved my skis to turn to face my fears, the obstruction was gone and so was Mr. Blackstone. So there I was again, staring into nothingness with only a mountain of snow for company and feeling stupid once more. I swore to myself that if I saw him again, I would give him a piece of my mind—how dare he quit so soon. One minute more and I would have caved in, and he could have fucked me in my ears if he had a mind to.

I headed down the slope, and at the very foot, I tripped, stumbled, rolled, and landed in a large bed of snow with my skis buried. I tried to stand, but that was impossible. I knew that I had sprained my ankle. Looking around, I didn't see anyone. I panicked, and screamed, "Hello!

I need help, I'm hurt!" Before I could yell again, standing in front of me was the extraordinary, handsome Mr. Black.

He rushed over to me, dug me out with a small shovel he carried somewhere, unfastened my skis, and lifted me like a doll. Cradled in his arms, I ceased to breathe. Gazing into my eyes, he asked, "Are you hurt?"

"It's my ankle." He touched it gently. I screamed, not from pain, but from desperately wanting his attention.

"You can't take pain. Pain can be exciting and satisfying," he said, flashing a smile. "You know childbirth is painful and satisfying."

"What did you say?" I always missed his cues.

"I guess we can't have children," he said, passing a dark, teasing smirk along his mouth while not taking his eyes off me. His gaze unnerved me. "I can carry you to my cabin. It's near. You're so light." I felt incredibly light, or I was incredibly stupid. He could be some kind of serial killer, or worse, a man who would make love to me and never see me again. Nevertheless, I felt comfortable in his arms, like I belonged there.

Stopping at a large house built with logs, with care Max walked up the stone stairs with me in his arms to this unbelievable redwood cabin in the middle of the snow and the mountains. I had never seen a house of that magnitude. It was built on a mountain with boulders as steps. Strong floor-to-ceiling glass windows surrounded the house, giving a panoramic view of everything for miles. The cabin was breathtaking, and it matched the owner—rich, beautiful, strong, and different.

We entered the house, and I looked around mystified at the decor. The foyer, wide as a museum's foyer, had numerous gray leather chairs placed facing the windows, and large paintings lined the walls. The house stood half on the mountain and half on large pillars, the kind you found under bridges. "This place is beautiful."

"You are beautiful," he said, making me uncomfortable. Looking around, I spied a roaring fire.

"Oh I love a fire," I said. He placed me in a large, cream leather chair near the huge fireplace, then picked up a log and fed the fire. It must have been his favorite chair because it sat alone with a large table nearby, with books and a small crystal chess set sitting on it. He watched deliberately as I acted like a little girl who had never had anything or been anywhere, and if he thought that, he would be right. Trying to stand, I wobbled. He rushed to me and knelt, looking up at me. "You can't walk on that leg. I will have the doctor here to examine it." His voice was commanding and strong.

"What about my job?"

"Joshua can get someone to replace you until you are fit for work. Remember they work for me and so do you, so relax and let me pamper you." My mind began to work overtime, trying to figure out what it was he was after and why me. He stood, walked away, turned, smiled, and strutted into an area that appeared to be a kitchen. Then he came back moments later with a bottle of wine, two glasses, and a tin of beluga caviar.

I wrinkled my nose at the caviar, and Max looked at me, confused. "Is something wrong, Alex?" I love the way the sound of my name dripped from his lips—so authoritative, so masculine. No man had ever called me Alex; they always wanted to feminize Alexander. My parents named me after Alexander the Great, the great conqueror.

"Drinking wine is not good for me; I have a low tolerance for wine, and I'll pass on the caviar, it's an acquired taste," I said, looking at him and thinking I had said something interesting. But the truth was I had never had caviar. I could tell by his smile and arched eyebrow that I wasn't fooling him.

"Oh, you are one of those," he said, staring as if he had seen an alien. "After today with your ankle, I thought you needed a drink. And the caviar, I'll get rid of it. I'll have my cook make you something more familiar." He scooped up the silver tray, holding the tin of caviar, with silver matching spoons, and disappeared into the kitchen. Then he returned looking disappointed and vulnerable. "I instructed my chef to make you soup, a sandwich, and a salad. You do eat lettuce?"

"Mr. Blackstone, I'll have the wine..."

He interrupted, "Call me Maximilian or Max." He poured the wine, and I took a sip, and before I could finish it someone rang the bell. It was the doctor. He examined me and my ankle, massaged it, gave me some muscle relaxants, and said that I should stay off it for twenty-four hours and I would be good to go. Max didn't leave me. He sat and waited for the doctor to finish examining me. The last thing I remembered was looking into Max's beautiful face.

Waking in the middle of the night to the moonlight flowing through the picture windows, I worried because I had fallen asleep around a man I didn't know. Was it the wine, or did Mr. Black slip something into my drink? No, it was the meds. He didn't have to drug me; I would give myself freely and happily, and he knew it. I felt my clothing. I was wearing a white silk top and nothing else. I felt the bed; now I knew what black silk sheets felt like. I smiled. I guessed he liked black. Then in the moonlight I saw a tall figure standing in the doorway with his legs crossed, his hand on his hip. "Are you okay?"

"Who undressed me? How did you know my size?"

He answered one of my questions. "Me. We are adults, after all," he said, inching in my direction.

"We may be adults, but you are my employer," I said, wincing. "I'll never be able to look at you without feeling uncomfortable."

"Well, you will not have to see me again unless you want to." He strutted close to the bed and sat at the corner, staring down at me. "Do you find me attractive?"

"What kind of question is that?" *A blind woman would find him attractive just from his voice. Doesn't he know how handsome and sexy he is especially in the moonlight?*

"I was taken with you the moment I saw your beautiful face," he said with a secret smile.

You weren't looking at my face. It was my breasts, you sexy fuck. Was he serious? Maybe he was blind, and I hadn't noticed. Maybe he had a missing leg, or he was impotent, and he would seduce anyone he could fool. Why me?

All possibilities crossed my mind, but I concluded—I didn't care. He leaned over to kiss me. I leaned back, away from his full lips. "I don't think we should do this." *I'm going to, but I don't want to go easy.*

"I won't tell if you don't," he said with a gleeful smile.

"I'm not what you think I am," I said, trying for respectability.

"You are exactly what I think you are," he said with a twist of his head.

"Some kind of slut you can give wine to, and I'll do anything to be near a rich, good-looking guy like you."

"So, you find me appealing."

"Well, yes, in a kind of sexy, odd way."

"Now I'm sexy?" he questioned with a soft smile and glowing eyes. He moved closer and leaned in to me. I tried to move away, but he draped his muscular arm across my lap and trapped me.

"I didn't quite mean it like that."

"What if I told you that I'm attracted to you?" Mr. Black said, eyes penetrating my glance.

"What if I told you that I'm not attracted to you?" I said, wanting to take those words back the minute they slipped from my lips.

"Then I'm hurt. Feel my heart; it's broken." Mr. Black took my hand and placed it to his hard chest. I felt his heart beating quickly as he nudged his face closer to my neck. My body responded to his closeness. His hand pushed my hair to the side, and he planted kisses on my neck, on my chin, and on my lips.

First a soft kiss, then one on the nape of my neck. He placed his strong, manicured hand around my back to brace me, threading his other hand through my curly, unruly auburn hair. He said, "I'm turned on by your lips, which make me want to..." He didn't finish his thought.

He strummed his finger over my top lip. *Maybe it's too soon for him to say that he wants me to wrap my full lips around his hard dick.*

He passed his finger across my bottom lip, letting it linger, and his eyes were smoldering and dark. Then he took my fingers and placed them in his mouth. I stared as he kissed them, and then he closed his eyes and sucked them. I looked in wonder. I felt a tingle move down my breasts and settle on my clit, then continue to my toes. This type of foreplay was new to me. I felt intensely drawn to him like metal drawn to a magnet. There was something sinful about how he kissed my fingers, and then his lips found my mouth.

His tongue swirled around and sucked my tongue as long as he had sucked my finger. I tried to reciprocate, drawing in his tongue, but he was in control and sucked my mouth dry, determined to seduce me with his foreplay; I was more than determined to allow him.

Lowering his head to my neck, he softly nipped it. I felt the feeling in my folds. His hands grabbed both breasts, and his fingers squeezed my nipples until they rose and ached with pleasure. His eyes searched mine as he lay over me, biting my neck and squeezing my nipples harder. I didn't cry out because, surprisingly, I enjoyed the intensity of his lovemaking. His gaze locked on me, and he must have seen in my eyes that I enjoyed every moment of his painful seduction.

"Does pain give you pleasure?" he said, meeting my gaze, and his fingers tightening on my nipples. *Yes, how does he know? I just found out.*

"Yes, yes, harder," I moaned, breathless. His eyes gleaming, he pinched my nipples harder. My breathing intensified.

His head moved down, his short, curly locks brushed against my breasts. I threaded my fingers through his hair and with his mouth he sucked each nipple, careful to tug each one in his teeth until they rose and turned red. I gave out a low moan. When I shouted it was with pleasure. He appeared hungry for a body, and that body lay in his bed, and it was mine.

I felt as if I had won the lottery. I was a lucky fuck for the day.

I had compromised my beliefs for that beautiful man making a meal out of my breasts, gorging himself until he felt satisfied filled me with pleasure. He took them in his hands. "These are beautiful. I can't get enough of them," he said, stroking them forward, pinching each nipple as it met his fingers. "...and they are mine." A dark gleam settled in his eyes. A penetrating look caused me to pull the straps of the silk top down my hips, leaving the thong, a thin strip up my ass, masquerading as underwear.

He helped pull the top down, and looked on me with my breasts heaving up and down. He straddled me as his eyes searched every inch of my body, then he placed his large hands on both sides of the string, and with one jerk, the strings came undone and his gaze lowered and settled on my pubic hair.

"Let it grow. Don't shave it again," he demanded. Then sliding down my body slowly, stopping to place a warm kiss on my stomach, he parted my legs and dropped his magnificent face between them. His tongue searched my clit until he found the spot he had been looking for. He caught me by surprise. My legs trembled, but soon relaxed, and I opened them wide.

I carelessly draped my legs over his shoulders, which excited me as well as him, because he clutched them with both hands, never coming up for breath.

His head moved with the intensity and the rhythm of his tongue. I wanted to know how it felt to have a man eat me. I had heard about it, but I didn't know it was so pleasurable. His energy was boundless. His hands cupped my breasts, and his fingers pinched my nipples as he worked his tongue. He had mastered a rhythm with his lips, tongue, hands, and fingers—the epitome of extreme multitasking.

I had my first orgasm, and before I could yell I had another one. It was a terrific feeling, and I could not contain a scream of pleasure. With a smile on his face, he moved and eased his body up, gazing in my eyes. My hands trembled as I helped him remove his shirt and pants.

I took his dick into my hands. He looked at me, his eyes begging me to do something with it or to it. It was so hard when I placed it in my mouth, lying on my back. I feared that my mouth could not contain it.

He saw the panic in my eyes; I didn't want to do the wrong thing. I took it out. "I've never done this before," I said, looking up at Mr. Black.

"I know," he said softly.

How did he know? I asked myself. Now was not the time to analyze.

"I'll teach you. I'll teach you to satisfy me." Those words sounded promising. Maybe I wasn't a one-night stand after all, but I was certainly his cunt for the day. As he directed me to hold his warm dick in my hand, I clutched it gently. "No, you're holding it like you're afraid of it. Tighter."

Finally, I got it. I felt in control as he tilted his head back, moaning with pleasure. "Alex, yes, that's what I like. Now suck it hard. I don't want to fill your mouth with my come; I want to fill your pussy. I can't wait."

With little patience, I sucked the head of his penis; up and down my mouth took it in. I wanted to control that dark, handsome, sexy, and titillating love of my life, man of my dreams, fucking trouble, who had ruined me for other men.

I tasted a hint of warm fluid, dropping slow, drip by drip until he pulled his dick from my mouth, and he held it with a painful expression, then with his strong arms he lifted me up, facing him. With his head buried in my breasts, he whispered, "Put it in, Alex." I hesitated and my hands quivered at the thought of the pain his hot, wet penis would inflict on the walls of my vagina. I guided his hard penis into the mouth of my vagina and stopped. I glared at Mr. Black with panicked eyes.

"You're a virgin, I know. I'll be careful." His mouth locked around my nipple, his long arm reaching and his fingers finding my folds, sending a current shooting to my toes. He opened my wet folds and inserted a finger, another finger softly, then breached my wall. Taking his fingers out, he placed them to his nose and inhaled, then inserted them in his mouth on his tongue, and said, "It's your smell that turns me on. That smell tells me no man has been here."

As I held my breath, he plowed the tip of his heavy penis into my vagina, inch by inch, taking more of my opening until he reached a roadblock. Then with a quick thrust he filled my vagina, as if he had heard somewhere that to limit the pain and reach the summit of a mountain, he had to do it quickly.

The nerves of my clit came alive. I opened my mouth to scream, but his lips cupped it, and he sucked my tongue in, rendering me speechless as he arched his body deep into my opening. I became used to his incredible hard penis. I took it in easily; it was a good fit. I knew it and he knew it.

Overmatched by his incredible body, his incredible lovemaking, his incredible handsome face, I yielded everything to him.

His energy was boundless. "I need more." His glance lay on my body instead of my eyes. I didn't say a word. I was numb from the meds. But I knew what I was doing and where I was going.

He whispered, "I should have been gentle, but I couldn't help myself. Your virgin pussy was so sweet and irresistible." He looked like a child declaring that he could not resist a piece of candy.

Mr. Black's face softened, and enjoyment and pleasure took hold. I wanted to give him the pleasure of my body, so that he would never forget me. As he thrust his dick into me once more, I met it with enjoyment as I tried to find out just what turned on my gorgeous fuck of a man. My fingernails trailed up and down his back, until I found that he responded. "Fuck me, Alex. Never stop. I love you. You're mine, and I'm your first."

And you will be my only man. I don't want anyone but you. Ever! I thought.

He leaned his head back, and his breathing intensified. I worked my hips at each positive expression on his face. His animalistic moans caused me to thrust forward into him and milk his penis up and down with my tight cunt. His body shook violently with pleasure and his come slowly drained into me.

He pulled me close, and our eyes met as I lay with my head on his muscular arm. I looked around and saw a large moon casting light on his hard chest. He knew all about me, but I knew nothing of him, except that I loved him, and he said that he loved me. I wanted to believe him.

He turned to face me with his hands between my thighs. "Alex, you look so sexy. I want more of you." He nudged under me and stroked my behind. His gaze covered my body as he fought off sleep. But he wasn't successful, and sleep won out. I was too giddy to close my eyes. I just stared at him with his drop-dead looks and body. His arm draped across my stomach. I wondered how I had gotten so lucky. Though I realized that I had never been lucky. I turned, lying in his arms with my head on his chest, and I remained in a state of ignorant bliss.

⎯⎯⎯◉⎯⎯⎯

The End of Chapter 1: The Incredible Mr. Black
By Rachel E Rice

Don't miss out!

Visit the website below and you can sign up to receive emails whenever Rachel E Rice publishes a new book. There's no charge and no obligation.

https://books2read.com/r/B-A-ASU-JPOE

BOOKS 2 READ

Connecting independent readers to independent writers.

Did you love *Black Tie Affair*? Then you should read *One Desire*[1] by Rachel E Rice!

[2]

When Tyler Burns graduates from a prep school in New Jersey and is the valedictorian of her prestigious high school, she assumes that her working-class background will take her only so far. And it probably would have gotten her a working-class stiff like her father, but she gets more than she expects when she meets Brandon Charles, a Princeton graduate, hot as the noon-day sun, with his blue-green eyes, sexy good looks, and a body to bring her to her knees. It's no wonder he's engaged, and he's expected to marry within a week.

Tyler accepts a ride home with Brandon from the frat party, never intending to end up in his bed at his estate, but she does. And if things can't get worse it does. She stays with him for a week, and most of the

---

1. https://books2read.com/u/m2RNRm

2. https://books2read.com/u/m2RNRm

week is spent in bed. He promises her he will return once he calls off the wedding. And she believes him and waits for him, but he never returns that night, or the next, or the next.

Five years later, she has graduated from college, when Brandon strolls back into her life in a restaurant with a beautiful girl, and Tyler is their waitress.

Read more at www.rachel-e-rice.com.

Also by Rachel E Rice

Blackstone
The Incredible Mr. Black
Blackstone Complete 10 Books Dark Romance Series
Temptation In Black
Blackstone Series 4 Books Box Set
Submission To Black
Black Tie Affair
The Incredible Mr. Black Box Set
Mourning Becomes Black
Fade To Black
Back to Black
Black Tide
Black Swan
Blackout
Blackstone Series 6 Books Box Set

I Am The Night
I Am The Night

Insatiable

Insatiable: The Lone Werewolf finds his mate
Insatiable: A Werewolf's Hunger
Insatiable: A Werewolf's Wedding
Insatiable: The Werewolves' Challenge
Hunter's Moon
Moon Tide
Moon Rapture

Insatiable Werewolf Series
A Bride For A Werewolf: The Beginning
Thorn in Moonscape
Insatiable: Damon in Moonscape
A Werewolf's Passion
Moonscape Box Set

Night
I Am First Night
I Am Last Night

Obsession
Obsession: Warm Bodies,Cold Hearts
Naked Obsession
Burning Obsession

Seduction
Seduced By An Earl

The Captain

The Captain and The Virgin

The Soul of A Vampire

Soul of A Vampire

Soul of A Vampire Book 2

Soul of A Vampire Book 3

To kill a vampire

To Kill a Vampire

To Kill A Vampire

To Kill A Vampire

Standalone

Finding Summer

One Desire

Insatiable Box Set: Books 1-4

Hunter's Moon Box Set

Hunter's Moon Insatiable Series

Insatiable: Tracker #8

Soul of A Vampire Box Set

The Complete Insatiable Werewolf Bundle

The Complete Insatiable Werewolf Bundle

I Am The Night Box Set

A Vampire Bundle

A Vampire Bundle

I Am The Night Box Set
To Kill A Vampire Boxset
To kill A Vampire Boxset
A Complete Vampire Bundle

Watch for more at www.rachel-e-rice.com.

About the Author

Rachel E. Rice enjoys writing in different genres. As an Indie author she explores genres to find her voice. She has written contemporary romance, erotic romance, new adult, historical and science fiction.

When she's not writing she is reading poetry. She has a BA and is a member of Romance Writers of America.

Read more at www.rachel-e-rice.com.